Also by Brian Aldiss in Panther Science Fiction

Greybeard

Brian W. Aldiss

The Moment of Eclipse

Panther

Granada Publishing Limited
Published in 1973 by Panther Books Ltd
Frogmore, St Albans, Herts, AL2 2NF

First published in Great Britain by
Faber and Faber Ltd 1970
Copyright © Brian Aldiss 1969, 1970, 1970, 1969,
1968, 1967, 1969, 1967, 1966, 1965, 1968, 1968, 1968, 1969
This collection copyright © Brian W. Aldiss 1970

Made and printed in Great Britain by
Richard Clay (The Chaucer Press), Ltd
Bungay, Suffolk
Set in Linotype Plantin

Contents

POEM AT A LUNAR ECLIPSE

Thy shadow, Earth, from Pole to
    Central Sea,
Now steals along upon the Moon's
    meek shine
In even monochrome and curving line
Of imperturbable serenity.

How shall I link such sun-cast
    symmetry
With the torn troubled form I know
    as thine,
That profile, placid as a brow divine,
With continents of moil and misery?

And can immense Mortality but
    throw
So small a shade, and Heaven's high
    human scheme
Be hemmed within the coasts yon
    arc implies?

Is such the stellar gauge of earthly
    show,
Nation at war with nation, brains that
    teem,
Heroes, and women fairer than the
    skies?

THOMAS HARDY

Reprinted by kind permission of Macmillan & Co. Ltd.

Beautiful women with corrupt natures – they have always been my life's target. There must be bleakness as well as loveliness in their gaze: only then can I expect the mingled moment.

The mingled moment – it holds both terror and beauty. Those two qualities, I am aware, lie for most people poles apart. For me, they are, or can become, one! When they do, they coincide, ah ... then joy takes me! And in Christiania I saw many such instants promised.

But the one special instant of which I have to tell, when pain and rapture intertwined like two hermaphrodites, overwhelmed me not when I was embracing any lascivious darling but when – after long pursuit! – I paused on the very threshold of the room where she awaited me: paused and saw ... that spectre....

You might say that a worm had entered into me. You might say that there I spoke metaphorically, and that the worm perverting my sight and taste had crept into my viscera in childhood, had infected all my adult life. So it may be. But who escapes the maggot? Who is not infected? Who dares call himself healthy? Who knows happiness except by assuaging his illness or submitting to his fever?

This woman's name was Christiania. That she was to provoke in me years of pain and pursuit was not her wish. Her wish, indeed, was at all times the very opposite.

We met for the first time at a dull party being held at the Danish Embassy in one of the minor East European capitals. My face was known to her and, at her request, a mutual friend brought her over to meet me.

She was introduced as a poet – her second volume of poetry was just published in Vienna. My taste for poetry exhibiting attitudes of romantic agony was what attracted her to me in the first place; of course she was familiar with my work.

Although we began by addressing each other in German, I soon discovered what I had suspected from something in her looks and mannerisms, that Christiania was also Danish. We started to talk of our native land.

Should I attempt to describe what she looked like? Christiania was a tall woman with a slightly full figure; her face was perhaps a little too flat for great beauty, giving her, from certain angles, a look of stupidity denied by her conversation. At that time, she had more gleaming dark hair than the fashion of the season approved. It was her aura that attracted me, a sort of desolation in her smile which is, I fancy, a Scandinavian inheritance. The Norwegian painter Edvard Munch painted a naked Madonna once, haunted, suffering, erotic, pallid, generous of flesh, with death about her mouth; in Christiania, that madonna opened her eyes and breathed!

We found ourselves talking eagerly of a certain *camera obscura* that still exists in the Aalborghus, in Jutland. We discovered that we had both been taken there as children, had both been fascinated to see a panorama of the town of Aalborg laid out flat on a table through the medium of a small hole in the roof. She told me that that optical toy had inspired her to write her first poem; I told her that it had directed my interest to cameras, and thus to filming.

But we were scarcely allowed time to talk before we were separated by her husband. Which is not to say that with look and gesture we had not already inadvertently signalled to each other, delicately but unmistakably.

Inquiring about her after the party, I was told that she was an infanticide currently undergoing a course of mental treatment which combined elements of Eastern and Western thought. Later, much of this information proved to be false; but, at the time, it served to heighten the desires that our brief meeting had woken in me.

Something fatally intuitive inside me knew that at her hands, though I might find suffering, I would touch the two-faced ecstasy I sought.

At this period, I was in a position to pursue Christiania further; my latest film, *Magnitudes*, was completed, although I had still some editing to do before it was shown at a certain film festival.

It chanced also that I was then free of my second wife, that *svelte*-mannered Parsi lady, ill-omened star alike of my first film and my life, whose vast promised array of talents was too quickly revealed as little more than a glib tongue and an over-sufficient knowledge of tropical medicine. In that very month, our case had been settled and Sushila had retreated to Bombay, leaving me to my natural pursuits.

So I planned to cultivate my erotic garden again: and Christiania should be the first to flower in those well-tended beds.

Specialized longings crystallize the perceptions along the axes concerned: I had needed only a moment in Christiania's presence to understand that she would not scruple to be unfaithful to her husband under certain circumstances, and that I myself might provide such a circumstance; for those veiled grey eyes told me that she also had an almost intuitive grasp of her own and men's desires, and that involvement with me was far from being beyond her contemplation.

So it was without hesitation that I wrote to her and described how, for my next film, I intended to pursue the train of thought begun in *Magnitudes* and hoped to produce a drama of a rather revolutionary kind to be based on a sonnet of the English poet Thomas Hardy entitled 'At a Lunar Eclipse'. I added that I hoped her poetic abilities might be of assistance in assembling a script, and asked if she would honour me with a meeting.

There were other currents in my life just then. In particular, I was in negotiation through my agents with the Prime Minister of a West African republic who wished to entice me out to make a film of his country. Although I nourished an inclination to visit this strange part of the world where, it always seemed to me, there lurked in the very atmosphere a menace compounded of grandeur and sordidness which might be much to my taste, I was attempting to evade the Prime Minister's offer, generous though it was, because I suspected that he needed a conservative documentary director rather than an innovator, and was more concerned with the clamour of my reputation than its nature. However, he would not be shaken off, and I was avoiding a cultural attaché of his as eagerly as I was trying to ensnare – or be ensnared by – Christiania.

In eluding this gigantic and genial black man, I was thrown into the company of an acquaintance of mine at the university, a professor of Byzantine Art, whom I had known for many years. It was in his study, in the low quiet university buildings with windows gazing from the walls like deep-set eyes, that I was introduced to a young scholar called Petar. He stood at one of the deep windows in the study, looking intently into the cobbled street, an untidy young man in unorthodox clothes.

I asked him what he watched. He indicated an old newspaper-seller moving slowly along the gutter outside, dragging and being dragged by a dog on a lead.

'We are surrounded by history, monsieur! This building was erected by the Habsburgs; and that old man whom you see in the gutter believes himself to be a Habsburg.'

'Perhaps the belief makes the gutter easier to walk.'

'I'd say harder!' For the first time he looked at me. In those pale eyes I saw an aged thing, although at the start I had been impressed by his extreme youth. 'My mother believes – well, that doesn't matter. In this gloomy city, we are all surrounded by the shadows of the past. There are shutters at all our windows.'

I had heard such rhetoric from students before. You find later they are reading Schiller for the first time.

My host and I fell into a discussion concerning the Hardy sonnet; in the middle of it, the youth had to take his leave of us; to visit his tutor, he said.

'A frail spirit, that, and a tormented one,' commented my host. 'Whether he will survive his course here without losing his mental stability, who can say. Personally, I shall be thankful when his mother, that odious woman, leaves the city; her effect on him is merely malevolent.'

'Malevolent in what respect?'

'It is whispered that when Petar was thirteen years old – of course, I don't say there's any truth in the vile rumour – when he was slightly injured in a road accident, his mother lay beside him – nothing unnatural in that – but the tale goes that unnatural things followed between them. Probably all nonsense, but certainly he ran away from home. His poor father, who is a public figure – these nasty tales always centre round public figures —'

Feeling my pulse rate beginning to mount, I inquired the family name, which I believe I had not been given till then. Yes! The pallid youth who felt himself surrounded by the shadows of the past was her son, Christiania's son! Naturally, this evil legend made her only the more attractive in my eyes.

At that time I said nothing, and we continued the discussion of the English sonnet which I was increasingly inspired to film. I had read it several years before in an Hungarian translation and it had immediately impressed me.

To synopsize a poem is absurd; but the content of this sonnet was to me as profound as its grave and dignified style. Briefly, the poet watches the curved shadow of Earth steal over the moon's surface; he sees that mild profile and is at a loss to link it with the continents full of trouble which he knows the shadow represents; he wonders how the whole vast scene of human affairs can come to throw so small a shade; and he asks himself if this is not the true gauge, by any outside standard of measurement, of all man's hopes and desires? So truly did this correspond with my own life-long self-questionings, so nobly was it cast, that the sonnet had come to represent one of the most precious things I knew; for this reason I wished to destroy it and reassemble it into a series of visual images that would convey precisely the same shade of beauty and terror allied as did the poem.

My host, however, claimed that the sequence of visual images I had sketched to him as being capable of conveying this mysterious sense fell too easily into the category of science-fiction, and that what I required was a more conservative approach – conservative and yet more penetrating, something more inward than outward; perhaps a more classical form for my romantic despair. His assertions angered me. They angered me, and this I realized even at the time, because there was the force of truth in what he said; the trappings should not be a distraction from but an illumination of the meaning. So we talked for a long time, mainly of the philosophical problems involved in representing one set of objects by another – which is the task of all art, the displacement without which we have no placement. When I left the university, it was wearily. I felt a sense of despair at the sight of dark falling and another day completed with my life incomplete.

Halfway down the hill, where a shrine to the virgin stands within the street wall, Petar's old news-vendor loitered, his shabby dog at his feet. I bought a paper from him, experiencing a tremor at the thought of how his image, glimpsed from the deep-set eye of the university, had been intertwined in my cogitations with the image of that perverted madonna whose greeds, so hesitatingly whispered behind her long back, reached out even to colour the imaginings of dry pedants like my friend in his learned cell!

And, as if random sequences of events were narrative in the mind of some super-being, as if we were no more than parasites in the head of a power to which Thomas Hardy himself might have yielded credulity, when I reached my hotel, the vendor's newspaper folded unopened under my arm, it was to find, in the rack of the ill-lit foyer, luminous, forbidding, crying aloud, silent, a letter from Christiania awaiting me. I knew it was from her! We had our connection!

Dropping my newspaper into a nearby waste bin, I walked upstairs carrying the letter. My feet sank into the thick fur of the carpet, slowing my ascent, my heart beat unmuffled. Was not this – so I demanded of myself afterwards! – one of those supreme moments of life, of pain and solace inseparable? For whatever was in the letter, it was such that, when revealed, like a fast-acting poison inserted into the bloodstream, would convulse me into a new mode of feeling and behaving.

I knew I would have to have Christiania, knew it even by the violence of my perturbation, greater than I had expected; and knew also that I was prey as well as predator. Wasn't that the meaning of life, the ultimate displacement? Isn't – as in the English sonnet – the great also the infinitely small, and the small also the infinitely great.

Well, once in my room, I locked the door, laid the envelope on a table and set myself down before it. I slit the envelope with a paper knife and withdrew her – her! – letter.

What she said was brief. She was much interested in my offer and the potential she read in it. Unfortunately, she was leaving Europe at the end of the week, the day after the morrow, since her husband was taking up an official post in Africa on behalf of his government. She regretted that our acquaintance would not deepen.

I folded the letter and put it down. Only then did I appreciate the writhe in the serpent's tail. Snatching up the letter again, I re-read it. She and her husband – yes! – were taking up residence in the capital city of that same republic with whose Prime Minister I had been long in negotiation. Only that morning had I written to his cultural attaché to announce finally that the making of such a film as he proposed was beyond my abilities and interests!

That night, I slept little. In the morning, when friends called upon me, I had my man tell them I was indisposed; and indisposed I was; indisposed to act; yet indisposed to let slip this opportunity. It was perversity, of course, to think of following this woman, this perverted madonna, to another continent; there were other women with whom the darker understandings would flow if I merely lifted the somewhat antique phone by my bedside. And it was perhaps perversity that allowed me to keep myself in indecision for so long.

But by afternoon I had decided. From a lunar distance, Europe and Africa were within the single glance of an eye; my fate was equally a small thing; I would follow her by the means so easily awaiting me.

Accordingly, I composed a letter to the genial black attaché, saying that I regretted my decision of yesterday, explaining how it had been instrumental in moving my mind in entirely the opposite direction, and announcing that I now wished to make the proposed film. I said I would be willing to leave for his native country with camera team and secretaries as soon as possible. I requested him to favour me with an early appointment. And I had this letter delivered by hand there and then.

There followed a delay which I weathered as best I could. The next two days I spent shut in the offices I had hired in a quiet part of the city, editing *Magnitudes*. It would be a satisfactory enough film, but already I saw it merely – as is the way with creative artists – as pointing towards the next work. Images of Africa already began to steal upon my brain.

At the end of the second day, I broke my solitude and sought out a friend. I confided to him my anger that the attaché had not condescended to give me a reply when I was so keen to get away. He laughed.

'But your famous attaché has returned home in disgrace! He was found robbing the funds. A lot of them are like that, I'm afraid! Not used to authority! It was all over the evening papers a couple of days ago – quite a scandal! You'll have to write to your Prime Minister.'

Now I saw that this was no ordinary affair. There were lines of magnetism directed towards the central attraction, just as

Remy de Gourmont claims that the markings on the fur of certain luxurious female cats run inescapably towards their sexual quarters. Clearly, I must launch myself into this forceful pattern. This I did by writing hastily – hastily excusing myself from my friend's presence – to the distant statesman in the distant African city, towards which, on that very evening, my maligned lady was making her way.

Of the awful delays that followed, I shall not speak. The disgrace of the cultural attaché (and it was not he alone who had been disgraced) had had its repercussions in the far capital, and my name, becoming involved, was not sweetened thereby. Finally, however, I received the letter I awaited, inviting me to make the film in my own terms, and offering me full facilities. It was a letter that would have made a less perverse man extremely happy!

To make my arrangements to leave Europe, to brief my secretary, and settle certain business matters took me a week. In that time, the distinguished film festival was held, and *Magnitudes* enjoyed from the critics just such a reception as I had anticipated; that is to say, the fawners fawned and the sneerers sneered, and both parties read into it many qualities that were not there, ignoring those that were – one even saw it as a retelling of the myth of the wanderings of Adam and Eve after their expulsion from Eden! Truly, the eyes of critics, those prideful optics, see only what they wish to see!

All irritations were finally at an end. With an entourage of five, I climbed aboard a jet liner scheduled for Lagos.

It seemed then that the climactic moment of which I was in search could not be far distant, either in time or space. But the unforeseen interposed.

When I arrived at my destination, it was to discover the African capital in an unsettled state, with demonstrations and riots every day and curfews every night. My party was virtually confined to its hotel, and the politicians were far too involved to bother about a mere film-maker!

In such a city, none of the pursuits of man are capable of adequate fulfilment: except one. I well recall being in Trieste when that city was in a similar state of turmoil. I was then undergoing a painful and exquisite love affair with a woman almost twice my age – but my age then was half what it now is!

– and the disruptions and dislocations of public life, the mysterious stoppages and equally mysterious pandemoniums that blew in like the *bora*, gave a delectable contrapuntal quality to the rhythms of private life, and to those unnerving caesuras which are inescapable in matters involving a beautiful married woman. So I made discreet inquiries through my own country's embassy for the whereabouts of Christiania.

The republic was in process of breaking in half, into Christian South and Muslim North. Christiania's husband had been posted to the North and his wife had accompanied him. Because of the unrest, and the demolition of a strategic bridge, there was no chance of my following them for some while.

It may appear as anti-climax if I admit that I now forgot about Christiania, the whole reason for my being in that place and on that continent. Nevertheless, I did forget her; our desires, particularly the desires of creative artists, are peripatetic: they submerge themselves sometimes unexpectedly and we never know where they may appear again. My imp of the perverse descended. For me the demolished bridge was never rebuilt.

Once the Army decided to support the government (which it did as soon as two of its colonels were shot), the riots were quelled. Although the temper of the people was still fractious, some sort of order was restored. I was then escorted about the locality. And the full beauty and horror of the city – and of its desolated hinterland – were rapidly conveyed to me.

I had imagined nothing from West Africa. Nobody had told me of it. And this was precisely what attracted me now, as a director. I saw that here was fresh territory from which a raid on the inarticulate might well be made. The images of beauty-in-despair for which I thirsted were present, if in a foreign idiom. My task was one of translation, of displacement.

So immersed was I in my work, that all the affairs of my own country, and of Europe, and of the western world where my films were acclaimed or jeered, and of the whole globe but this little troubled patch (where, in truth, the preoccupations of all the rest were echoed) were entirely set aside. My sonnet was here; here, I would be able to provide more than a dead gloss on Hardy's sonnet. The relativity of importance was here brought to new parameters!

As the political situation began to improve, so I began to work further afield, as if the relationship between the two events was direct. A reliable Ibo hunter was placed at my disposal.

Although man was my subject and I imagined myself not to be interested in wild life, the bush strangely moved me. I would rise at dawn, ignoring the torment of early-stirring flies, and watch the tremendous light flood back into the world, exulting to feel myself simultaneously the most and least important of creatures. And I would observe – and later film – how the inundating light launched not only flies but whole villages into action.

There was a vibrance in those dawns and those days! I still go cold to think of it.

Suppose – how shall we say it? – suppose that while I was in Africa making *Some Eclipses*, one side of me was so fully engaged (a side never before exercised in open air and sunlight) that another aspect of myself slumbered? Having never met with any theory of character which satisfied me, I cannot couch the matter in any fashionable jargon. So let me say brutally: the black girls who laid their beauty open to me stored in their dark skins and unusual shapes and amazing tastes enough of the unknown to hold the need for deeper torments at bay. In those transitory alliances, I exorcized also the sari-clad ghost of my second wife.

I became temporarily almost a different person, an explorer of the psyche in a region where before me others of my kind had merely shot animals; and I was able to make a film that was free from my usual flights of perversity.

I know that I created a masterpiece. By the time *Some Eclipses* was a finished masterpiece, and I was back in Copenhagen arranging details of premiers, the regime that had given me so much assistance had collapsed; the Prime Minister had fled to Great Britain; and Muslim North had cut itself off from Christian South. And I was involved with another woman again, and back in my European self, a little older, a little more tired.

Not until two more years had spent themselves did I again cross the trail of my perverted madonna, Christiania. By then, the lines of the magnet seemed to have disappeared altogether: and, in truth, I was never to lie with her as I so deeply schemed to do: but magnetism goes underground and surfaces in strange places; the invisible suddenly becomes flesh before our eyes; and terror can chill us with more power than beauty knows.

My fortunes had now much improved – a fact not unconnected with the decline of my artistic powers. Conscious that I had for a while said what I needed to say, I was now filming coloured narratives, employing some of my old tricks in simpler form, and, in consequence, was regarded by a wide public as a daring master of effrontery. I lived my part, and was spending the summer sailing in my yacht, *The Fantastic Venus*, in the Mediterranean.

Drinking in a small French restaurant on a quayside, my party was diverted by the behaviour of a couple at the next table, a youth quarrelling with a woman, fairly obviously his paramour, and very much his senior. Nothing about this youth revived memories in me; but suddenly he grew tired of baiting his companion and marched over to me, introducing himself as Petar and reminding me of our one brief meeting, more than three years ago. He was drunk, and not charming. I saw he secretly disliked me.

We were more diverted when Petar's companion came over and introduced herself. She was an international film personality, a star, one might say, whose performances of recent years had been confined more to the bed than the screen. But she was piquant company, and provided a flow of scandal almost unseemly enough to be indistinguishable from wit.

She set her drunken boy firmly in the background. From him, I was able to elicit that his mother was staying near by, at a noted hotel. In that corrupt town, it was easy to follow one's inclinations. I slipped away from the group, called a taxi, and was soon in the presence of an unchanged Christiania, breathing the air that she breathed. Heavy lids shielded my madonna's eyes. She looked at me with a fateful gaze that seemed to have shone on me through many years. She was an echo undoubtedly of something buried, something to resurrect and view as closely as possible.

'If you chased me to Africa, it seems somewhat banal to catch up with me in Cannes,' she said.

'It is Cannes that is banal, not the event. The town is here for our convenience, but we have had to wait on the event.'

She frowned down at the carpet, and then said, 'I am not sure what event you have in mind. I have no events in mind. I am simply here with a friend for a few days before we drive on to somewhere quieter. I find living without events suits me particularly well.'

'Does your husband —'

'I have no husband. I was divorced some while ago – over two years ago. It was scandalous enough: I am surprised you did not hear.'

'No, I didn't know. I must still have been in Africa. Africa is practically soundproof.'

'Your devotion to that continent is very touching. I saw your film about it. I have seen it more than once, I may confess. It is an interesting piece of work – of art, perhaps one should say only —'

'What are your reservations?'

She said, 'For me it was incomplete.'

'I also am incomplete. I need you for completion, Christiania – you who have formed a spectral part of me for so long!' I spoke then, burningly, and not at all as obliquely as I had intended.

She was before me, and again the whole pattern of life seemed to direct me towards her mysteries. But she was there with a friend, she protested. Well, he had just had to leave Cannes on a piece of vital business (I gathered he was a minister in a certain government, a man of importance), but he would be back on the morning plane.

So we came gradually round – now my hands were clasping hers – to the idea that she might be entertained to dinner on *The Fantastic Venus*; and I was careful to mention that next to my cabin was an empty cabin, easily prepared for any female guest who might care to spend the night aboard before returning home well before any morning planes circled above the bay.

And so on, and so on.

There can be few men – women either – who have not experienced that particular mood of controlled ecstasy awakened by the promise of sexual fulfilment, before which obstacles are nothing and the logical objections to which we normally fall victim less than nothing. Our movements at such times are scarcely our own; we are, as we say, possessed: that we may later possess.

A curious feature of this possessed state is that afterwards we recall little of what happened in it. I recollect only driving fast through the crowded town and noticing that a small art theatre was showing *Some Eclipses*. That fragile affair of light and shadow had lasted longer, held more vitality, than the republic about which it centred! I remember thinking how I would like to humble the arrogant young Petar by making him view it – 'one in the eye for him', I thought, amused by the English phrase, envious of what else his eyes might have beheld.

Before my obsessional state, all impediments dissolved. My party was easily persuaded to savour the pleasures of an evening ashore; the crew, of course, was happy enough to escape. I sat at last alone in the centre of the yacht, my expectations spreading through it, listening appreciatively to every quiet movement. Music from other vessels in the harbour reached me, seeming to confirm my impregnable isolation.

I was watching as the sun melted across the sea, its vision hazed by cloud before it finally blinked out and the arts of evening commenced. That sun was flinging, like a negative of itself, our shadow far out into space: an eternal blackness trailing after the globe, never vanquished, a blackness parasitic, claiming half of man's nature!

Even while these and other impressions of a not unpleasant kind filtered through my mind, sudden trembling overcame me. Curious unease seized my senses, an indescribable *frisson*. Clutching the arms of my chair, I had to fight to retain consciousness. The macabre sensation that undermined my being was – this phrase occurred to me at the time – that *I was being silently inhabited*, just as I at that moment silently inhabited the empty ship.

What a moment for ghosts! When my assignation was for the flesh!

Slightly recovering from the first wave of fear, I sat up. Distant music screeched across the slaty water to me. As I passed a hand over my bleared vision, I sat that my palm bore imprinted on it the pattern of the rattan chair arm. This reinforced my sense of being at once the host to a spectral presence and myself insubstantial, a creature of infinite and dislocated space rather than flesh.

That terrible and cursed malaise, so at variance with my mood preceding it! And even as I struggled to free myself from it, my predatorial quarry stepped aboard. The whole yacht subtly yielded to her step, and I heard her call my name.

With great effort, I shook off my eerie mood and moved to greet her. Although my hand was chill as I clutched her warm one, Christiania's imperious power beamed out at me. The heavy lids of Munch's voluptuous madonna opened to me and I saw in that glance that this impressive and notorious woman was also unfolded to my will.

'There is something Venetian about this meeting,' she said, smiling. 'I should have come in a domino!'

The trivial pleasantry attached itself to my extended sensibilities with great force. I imagined that it could be interpreted as meaning that she acted out a role; and all my hopes and fears leaped out to conjure just what sort of a role, whether of ultimate triumph or humiliation, I was destined to play in her fantasy!

We talked fervently, even gaily, as we went below and sat in the dim-lit bar in the stern to toast each other in a shallow drink. That she was anxious I could see, and aware that she had taken a fateful step in so compromising herself: but this anxiety seemed part of a deeper delight. By her leaning towards me, I could interpret where her inclinations lay; and so, by an easy gradation, I escorted her to the cabin next to mine.

But now, again, came that awful sense of being occupied by an alien force! This time there was pain in it and, as I switched on the wall-lights, a blinding spasm in my right eye, almost as though I had gazed on some forbidden scene.

I clutched at the wall. Christiania was making some sort of absurd condition upon fulfilment of which her favours would be bestowed; perhaps it was some nonsense about her son, Petar; at the same time, she was gesturing for me to come to her. I made some excuse – I was now certain that I was about to disintegrate – I stammered a word about preparing myself in the next cabin – begged her to make herself comfortable for a moment, staggered away, shaking like an autumn leaf.

In my cabin – rather, in the bathroom, jetty lights reflected from the surface of the harbour waters projected a confused imprint of a porthole on the top of the door. Wishing for no other illumination, I crossed to the mirror to stare at myself and greet my haggard face with questioning.

What ailed me What sudden illness, what haunting, had taken me – overtaken me – at such a joyful moment?

My face stared back at me. And then: *my sight was eclipsed from within. . . .*

Nothing can convey the terror of that experience! Something that moved, that moved across my vision as steadily and as irretrievably as the curved shadow in Hardy's sonnet. And, as I managed still to stare at my gold-haloed face in the mirror, I *saw* the shadow move in my eye, traverse my eyeball, glide slowly – so eternally slowly! – across the iris from north to south.

Exquisite physical and psychological pain were mine. Worse, I was pierced through by the dread of death – by what I imagined a new death: and I saw vividly, with an equally pain-laden inner eye, all my vivid pleasures, carnal and spiritual alike, and all my gifts, brought tumbling into that ultimate chill shadow of the grave.

There at that mirror, as if all my life I had been rooted there, I suffered alone and in terror, spasms coursing through my frame, so far from my normal senses that I could not hear even my own screams. And the terrible thing moved over my eyeball and conquered me!

For some while, I lay on the floor in a sort of swoon, unable either to faint or to move.

When at last I managed to rise, I found I had dragged myself into my cabin. Night was about me. Only phantoms of light, reflections of light, chased themselves across the ceiling and disappeared. Faintly, feebly, I switched on the electric light and once more examined the trespassed area of my sight. The terrible thing was transitory. There was only soreness where it had been, but no pain.

Equally, Christiania had left – fled; I learned later, at my first screams, imagining in guilty dread perhaps that her husband had hired an assassin to watch over her spoiled virtue!

So I too had to leave! The yacht I could not tolerate for a day more! But nothing was tolerable to me, not even my own body; for the sense of being inhabited was still in me. I felt myself a man outside society. Driven by an absolute desperation of soul, I went to a priest of that religion I had left many years ago; he could only offer me platitudes about bowing to God's will. I went to a man in Vienna whose profession was to cure sick minds; he could talk only of guilt-states.

Nothing was tolerable to me in all the places I knew. In a spasm of restlessness, I chartered a plane and flew to that African country where I had once been happy. Though the republic had broken up, existing now only in my film, the land still remained unaltered.

My old Ibo hunter was still living; I sought him out, offered him good pay, and we disappeared into the bush as we had previously done.

The thing that possessed me went too. Now we were becoming familiar, it and I. I had an occasional glimpse of it, though never again so terrifyingly as when it eclipsed my right eye. It was peripatetic, going for long submerged excursions through my body, suddenly to emerge just under the skin, dark, shadowy, in my arm, or breast or leg, or once – and there again were terror and pain interlocked – in my penis.

I developed also strange tumours, which swelled up very rapidly to the size of a hen's egg, only to disappear in a couple of days. Sometimes these loathsome swellings brought fever, always pain. I was wasted, useless – and used.

These horrible manifestations I tried my best to keep hidden from everyone. But, in a bout of fever, I revealed the swellings to my faithful hunter. He took me – I scarcely knowing where I went – to an American doctor who practised in a village near by.

'No doubt about it!' said the doctor, after an almost cursory examination. 'You have a loiasis infestation. It's a parasitic worm with a long incubation period – three or more years. But you weren't in Africa that long were you?'

I explained that I had visited these parts before.

'It's an open-and-shut case, then! That's when you picked up the infection.'

I could only stare at him. He belonged in a universe far from mine, where every fact has one and only one explanation.

'The loiasis vector is a blood-sucking fly,' he said. 'There are billions of them in this locality. They hit maximum activity at dawn and late afternoon. The larval loiasis enters the blood-stream when the fly bites you. Then there is a three–four year incubation period before the adult stage emerges. It's what you might call a tricky little system!'

'So I'm tenanted by a worm, you say!'

'You're acting as unwilling host to a now adult parasitic worm of peripatetic habit and a known preference for subcu-taneous tissue. It's the cause of these tumours. They're a sort of allergic reaction.'

'So I don't have what you might call a psychosomatic dis-order?'

He laughed. 'The worm is real right enough. What's more, it can live in your system up to fifteen years.'

'Fifteen years! I'm to be haunted by this dreadful succubus for fifteen years!'

'Not a bit of it! We'll treat you with a drug called diethyl-carbamazine and you'll soon be okay again.'

That marvellous optimism – 'soon be okay again!' – well, it was justified in his sense, although his marvellous drug had some unpleasant side effects. Of that I would never complain; all of life has unpleasant side effects. It may be – and this is a supposition I examine in the film I am at present making – that consciousness itself is just a side effect, a trick of the light, as it were, as we humans, in our ceaseless burrowings, accidentally surface now and again into a position and a moment where our presence can influence a wider network of sensations.

In my dark subterranean wanderings, I never again met the fatal Christiania (to whom my growing aversion was not strong enough to attract me further!); but her son, Petar, sports in the wealthier patches of Mediterranean sunshine still, surfacing to public consciousness now and again in magazine gossip columns.

The ruined hillside above the lake was an idyllic place for conversation and fete. We could see the town but not the palace, and the river beyond the town, and flowers grew in the warm bank on which we sat. The pines were shattered, the dells incredible, the scents of acacia all that mid-June could demand. I had forgotten my guitar, and my stout friend Portinari insisted on wearing his scarlet conversing-jacket.

So he was conversing on grandiose scarlet themes, and I was teasing him. 'Mankind lives between animal and intellectual worlds by reason of its cerebral inheritance. I am mathematician and scholar. I am also dog and ape.'

'Do you live in the rival worlds alternately or both in the same moment?'

He gestured, looking down the hillside to where young men fought with yellow poles. 'I am not speaking of rival worlds. They are complementary, one to another, mathematician, scholar, dog, ape, all in one capacious brain.'

'You surprise me.' I took care to look unsurprised as I spoke. 'The mathematician must find the antics of the dog tedious, and does not the ape revolt against the scholar?'

'They all fight it out in bed,' said Clyton, cuttingly. We thought he had left our conversation to our own devices, for he squatted at our feet under one of the shattered tombstones, presenting the fantastic patterns of his satin-covered back to us as he examined the ancient graves.

'They fight it out in science,' offered Portinari: less a correction than a codicil.

'They truce it out in art,' I said: less a codicil than a coda.

'How about this fossil of art?' Clyton asked. He rose, smiling at us under his punchinello mask, and held out the fragment of tomb he had been scrutinizing.

It bore a human figure crudely outlined in stone, blurred further by lichen, one patch of which had, with mycotic irony, provided the figure with a fuzz of yellowing pubic hair. In one hand the figure clutched an umbrella; the other hand, offered palm outwards, was enlarged grotesquely.

'Is he supplicating?' I asked.

'Or welcoming?' Portinari asked.

'If so, welcoming what?'

'Death?'

'He's testing for rain. Hence the umbrella,' Clyton said. We laughed.

Through the low hills, screams rang.

Nothing here attracted life, for the drought of some centuries' standing had long since withered all green things. The calm was the calm of paralysis, which even the screams could not break. Through the hills, making for the edge of a distant horizon, ran the double track of a railway line. Along this line, a giant steam locomotive fled, screaming. Behind it, pursuing, came the carnivores.

There were six carnivores, their headlights blazing. They were now almost abreast of their quarry. Their klaxons echoed as they called to each other. It could be only a short while before they pulled their victim down.

The locomotive was untiring. For all its superb strength, it could not outdistance the carnivores. Nor was there any help for it here; the nearest station was still many hundreds of miles away.

Now the leading carnivore was level with its cab. In desperation, the locomotive suddenly flung itself sideways, off the confining rails, and charged into the dried river bed that lay on one side. The carnivores halted for a moment, then swung to the side also and again roared in pursuit. Now the advantage was more than ever with them, for the locomotive's wheels sank into the ground.

In a few minutes, it was all over. The great beasts dragged down their prey. The locomotive keeled heavily on to its side, thrashing out vainly with its pistons. Undeterred, the carnivores hurled themselves on to its black and vibrating body.

Through the hills, screams rang.

Though the king had decreed a holiday, we still had our wards strapped to our wrists. I punched for Universal Knowledge and asked about rainfall in the area four centuries previously. No figures. Climate reckoned equable.

'Machines are so confoundedly imprecise,' I complained.

'But we live by imprecision, Bryan! That's how Portinari's mathematician and puppy dog manage to co-exist in his well-endowed head. We made the machines, so they bear our impress of imprecision.'

'They're binary. What's imprecise about either-or, on-off?'

'Surely either-or is the major imprecision! Mathematician-dog. Scholar-ape. Rain-fine. Life-death. It's not the imprecision in the things but in the hiatus between them, the dash between the either and the or. In that hiatus is our heritage. Our heritage the machines have inherited.'

While Clyton was saying this, Portinari was brushing away the pine-needles on the other side of the tomb (or perhaps I might make that stout friend of mine sound more mortal if I said on the *opposite* side of the tomb). A metal ring was revealed. Portinari pulled it, and dragged a picnic basket from the earth.

As we were exclaiming over the basket's contents, pretty Columbine arrived. She kissed us each in turn and offered to lay a picnic for us. From the top of the basket, she produced a snowy cloth and, spreading it out, commenced to arrange the viands upon it. Portinari, Clyton, and I stood about in pictur-esque attitudes and watched the four-man fliers flapping their way slowly across the blue sky above our heads.

Outside the wall of the town, a silver band played for the princess's birthday. Its notes came faintly up to us, preserved in the thin air. One could almost taste them, like the thin beaten sheets of silver in which duckling is cooked.

'It's so beautiful today – how fortunate we are that it will have an end. Permanent happiness lies only in the transitory.'

'You're changing the subject, Bryan,' Portinari said. 'You were being taxed on imprecision.'

I clutched my heart in horror. 'If I am to be taxed for im-precision, then it is not the subject but the king who must be changed!'

Just a fraction late, Clyton replied, 'Your tributary troubles make for streams of mirth.'

Columbine laughed prettily and curtsied to indicate that our spread was ready.

The savannas ended here, were superseded abruptly by a region of stone, a semi-desert place where few of the giant herbivores ever ventured. The same heavy sky lowered over all. Sometimes the rain fell for years at a time.

Compared with the slow herbivores, the carnivores were fleet. They ranged down their terrible black road, which cut through savanna and desert alike.

One lay by the edge of the roadside slowly devouring a two-legged thing, its engine purring. Fitful sun marked its flanks.

As we sat down to our picnic, removing our masks, one of the hill-dwarfs came springing up in his velvet and sat on the sward beside us, playing his electric dulcimer for Columbine to dance to. He had a face like a human foetus, hanging over the strings, but his voice was clear and true. He sang an old ditty of Caesura's:

> '*I listened to every phrase she uttered*
> *Knowing, knowing they'd be recorded only*
> *In my memory – and knowing, knowing my memory*
> *Would improve them all by and by....*'

To this strain, Columbine did a graceful dance, not without its own self-mocking quality. We watched as we ate iced melon and ginger, in which were embedded prawns, and silver carp and damson tart. Before the dance was over, boys in satins carrying banners and a tiny black girl with a tambor came scurrying out of the magnolia groves to listen to the music. With them on a chain they led a little green-and-orange dinosaur which waltzed about on its hind legs. We thought this party must be from the court.

A plump boy was with them. I remarked him first because he was dressed all in black; then I noticed the leathery flying creature on his shoulder. He could have been no more than twelve, yet was monstrously plump and evidently boasted abnormally large sexual appendages, for they were hung before him in a yellow bag. He gave us greeting, doffing his cap, and then stood with his back to the frolic, looking across the valley to the far woods and hills. He provided an agreeable foil to the merriment, which we watched as we ate.

Everyone pranced to the song of the hill-dwarf's dulcimer.

The carnivores ran along endless roads, indifferent to whether the land through which they passed was desert, savanna, or forest. They could always find food, so great was their speed.

The heavy skies overhead robbed the world of colour and time. The lumbering grass-eaters seemed almost motionless. Only the carnivores were bright and tireless, manufacturing their own time.

A group of them were converging on a certain crossroads in an area of heath. One of their number had made a kill. It was a big grey beast. Its radiator grill was bared in a snarl. It sprawled at its leisure on the roadside, devouring the body of a young female. Two others of her kind, freshly killed, lay nearby, to be dealt with at will.

This was long before internal parasites had labyrinthed their way into the mechanisms of eternity.

'Come now, Bryan,' Portinari said as he opened up a second bottle of new wine. 'Clyton here was quizzing you on imprecision. You twice evaded the point, and now pretend to be absorbed in the antics of these dancers!'

Clyton leaned back on one elbow, gesturing lordly in the air with a jellied chicken-bone. 'What with the smell of the acacia blossom and the tang of this new vintage, I've forgotten the point myself, Portinari, so we'll let Bryan off for once. He's free to go!'

'To be let off is not necessarily to be free,' I said. 'Besides, I am capable of liberating myself from any argument.'

'I believe truly you could slip out of a cage of words,' said Clyton.

'Why not? Because all sentences contain contradictions, as we all contain contradictions, in the way that Portinari is mathematician and dog, ape and scholar.'

'*All* sentences, Bryan?' Portinari asked, teasingly.

We smiled at each other, the way we did when preparing verbal traps for each other. The party of children from the court had gathered round to hear our talk, all except the plump boy dressed in black, who now leaned against an aspen trunk and regarded the blue distances of the landscape. With sweet gestures, the others lolled against one another to decide if we talked wisdom or nonsense.

Of course Columbine was not listening. More of the velvet-clad dwarfs had arrived. They were singing and dancing and making a great noise; only the first-comer of their tribe had laid down his dulcimer and was fondling and kissing the lovely bare shoulders of Columbine.

Still smiling, I passed my glass towards Portinari and he filled it to the brim. We were both of us relaxed but alert, coming to the test.

'How would you describe that action, Portinari?'

They all waited for his answer. Cautiously, smiling yet, he said, 'I shall not be imprecise, dear Bryan. I poured you some newly-bottled wine, that was all!'

A toad hopped under one of the broken tombstones. I could hear its progress, so quiet had our circle become.

' "I poured you some newly-bottled wine" ', I quoted. 'You provide a perfect contradiction, my friend, as I predicted. At the beginning of your sentence, you pour the wine, yet by the end of the sentence it is newly-bottled. Your sequence contradicts utterly your meaning. Your time-sense is so awry that you negate what you did in one breath!'

Clyton burst out laughing – even Portinari had to laugh – the children squeaked and fluttered – the dinosaur plunged – and as Columbine clapped her pretty hands in mirth, the hill-dwarf flipped out of her corsage the two generous orbs of her breasts. Clutching them, she jumped up and ran laughing through the trees towards the lake, her pet fawn following her, the dwarf chasing her.

Over the lush grass rain swept in curtains of moisture. It seemed to hang in the air rather than descend, to soak everything between ground and sky. It was an enormous summer shower, silent and fugitive; it had lasted for tens of thousands of years.

Occasionally the sun broke through clouds, and then the moving moistures of the air burst into violent colour, only to fade to a drab brass tint as the clouds healed their wound.

The metal beasts that drove through this perpetual shower hooted and snarled on their way. Outwardly, they shone as if impervious, paintwork and chromework as bright as knives; but, below their armour, the effects of the water, dashing up for ever from their spinning wheels, were lethal. Rust crept into every moving part, metal's cancer groping for the heart.

The cities where the beasts lived were surrounded by huge cemeteries. In the cemeteries, multitudinous carcasses, no longer to be feared, lapsed into ginger dust, into poor graves.

As we were draining the wine and eating the sweetmeats, the dwarfs and boys danced on the sward. Some of the youths leapt on their goose-planes and pedalled up above our heads for aerial jousting-matches. All the while, the black-clad plump boy stood in lonely contemplation. Portinari, Clyton, and I laughed and chatted, and flirted with some country wenches who passed by. I was pleased when Portinari explained my paradox of imprecision to them.

When the girls had gone, Clyton, rising, swept his cloak about him and suggested we should move back to the ferry.

'The sun inclines towards the west, my friends, and the hills grow brazen to meet its glare.' He gestured grandly at the sun. 'All its trajectory is dedicated, I am certain, towards proving Bryan's earlier aphorism, that the only permanent happiness lies in transitory things. It reminds us that this golden afternoon is merely of counterfeit gold, now wearing thin.'

'It reminds me that I'm wearing fat,' said Portinari, struggling up, belching, and smoothing his stomach.

I picked up Clyton's figured fragment from the tombstone and offered it to him.

'Yes, perhaps I'll keep this umbrella-bearing shade until I find someone to throw light on him.'

'Is he supplicating you to?' I asked.

'Or welcoming you to?' Portinari.

'He's testing for rain.' Clyton. We laughed again.

Almost hidden by a nauseous haze of its own manufacture, a pride of machines lay by the side of the road, feeding.

The road was like a natural feature. The great veldt, which stretched almost planet-wide, ended here at last. It appeared to terminate without reason. As inexplicably, the mountains began, rising from the dirt like icebergs from a petrified sea. They were still new and unsteady. The road ran along their base, a hem on the mighty skirt of plain.

It was a twenty-two lane highway, with provision for both mach-negative and mach-positive traffic. The pride lay in one of the infrequent rest-places, gorging itself on the soft red-centred creatures that rode in the machines. There were five machines in the pride, perpetually backing and revving engines as they scrambled for better positions.

Juice spurted from their radiator grills, streamed over their cowling, misted their windscreens. The tainted blue of their breath hung over them. They were devouring their young.

'So we retreat from our retreat!' said Clyton, shouldering his stone. The rabble still frolicked among the trees.

As we were moving off, it chanced I was just behind my friends. On impulse, I plucked the sleeve of the plump boy in black and asked him, 'May a stranger inquire what has pre-occupied your thoughts all through this sumptuous afternoon?'

When he turned his face to me and removed his mask, I saw how pale he was; the flesh of his body carried no echo on his face: it resembled a skull.

He looked at me long before he said, slowly, 'Perhaps truth is an accident.' And he cast his gaze to the ground.

His words caught me by surprise. I could find no rejoinder. perhaps because his manner was grave enough to forbid repartee.

Only as I turned to leave did he add, 'It may hap that you and your friends talked truth all afternoon-long by accident. Perhaps indeed our time-sense is awry. Perhaps the wine is never poured, or forever poured. Perhaps we are contradictions, each one in himself. Perhaps ... perhaps we are too imprecise to survive....'

His voice was low, and the other party was still making its merry noise – the dwarfs would continue to dance and frolic long after sunset. Only as I hurried away through the saplings after Portinari and Clyton did his words actually register on me: 'Perhaps we are too imprecise to survive....'

A melancholy thing to say on a gay day!

And there was the ferry, floating on the dark lake, screened by tall cypresses and so rather gloomy. But already lanterns twinkled along the shore, and I caught the sound of music and singing and laughter aboard. Back at the tavern, our sweethearts would be waiting for us, and our new play would open at midnight. I had my rôle by heart, I knew every word, I longed to walk out of the wings into the glittering lights, cynosure of all eyes. . . .

'Come on, my friend!' cried Portinari heartily, turning back from the throng and catching my arm. 'Look, my cousins are aboard – we shall have a merry trip homewards! Will you survive?'

Survive?

Survive?

Survive?

This was the way his wife's voice came to Tancred Frazer.

She visiphoned his world-code number from the cool hall in their country house situated in the depths of Hampshire, England. The vision and sound impulses were accepted by the local exchange and carried along co-axial cable to the Southampton main exchange, and from there broadcast to the transmitter at Goonhilly Down in Cornwall. From Goonhilly, the signal went up to Postbird III, the communications satellite, which promptly bounced it back to Earth again.

The signal was accepted at Calcutta. Here came the first delay – a wait of four and a half minutes before the call could be accepted by the Allahabad office, in the Province of Uttar Pradesh, in the heart of India. Finally, a relay clicked over on the automatic exchange, and the next link in the circuit was opened. After a brief delay, the call got as far as Faizabad, to the north of Allahabad.

At Faizabad, the automatic processes ceased. They were planned for installation there in 2001, the following year; but, since the official declaration of famine by the government, it looked as if the new exchange might have to wait. Meanwhile, the very pleasant operator on the board managed, after some minutes delay, to get the incoming call through to the village of Chandanagar, twenty miles away.

Chandanagar was small, and had remained insignificant for some thousands of years until the UN Famine Abatement Wing had arrived and set up its establishments in the semi-desert thereabouts. Chandanagar, in fact, could accept only the sound signal; it did not boast a microphoto-diode bankage capable of handling vision calls. So Chandanagar shuttled the sound signal only forward to UNFAW HQ.

The very pleasant operator at UNFAW HQ read back the world-code number, checked with a list, and said, 'Oh, you want the British Detachment! Tancred Frazer is with the British Detachment. They are about five miles from here, but I have a land-line. Hang on!'

He had a temporary line available. Leaning dangerously over

on his stool, he plugged in to an auxiliary board and cranked a handle with some vigour. A phone bell spluttered five miles away.

It rang in the front office of an air-conditioned building around which, for many miles in all directions, lay the heat-baked plain of the Ganges. Heavy on the plain lay the death that drought brought in its wake.

Tancred Frazer himself answered the phone when it splut-you suffer the malnutrition which brings all kinds of shadow-tered the third time, and so was able to hear his wife's voice as she spoke from the cool lounge of their house in Hampshire.

For all the glad noises they made at each other, their conversation went haltingly.

'The daffodils were over by the end of the first week in April.'

They seemed very soon to get down to unimportant things.

'Late for daffodils, wasn't it?'

the flower shall die and also the seed thereof but some flowers

'No, darling, very early. There *is* something the matter, isn't there? Do please tell me if there is. You know I shall only worry. Is the sight of all those poor starving people getting you down?'

He held a hand to his brow and said, 'No, I'm fine. Kathie —' But he could not bring himself to make any declarations of affection; that would have been too false, even for him, in the circumstances.

'I'm going to ring off and worry if you don't tell me, you know.'

'I'm being bombarded by voices,' reluctantly.

'You're eating buns and what? This is a terrible line.'

'I said I'm being bombarded by voices in my head – your voice and all these pathetic people here.'

'Poor darling! It's the heat, I'm sure. Is it awfully hot in Chandanagar now?'

That was safer; they were getting back to the weather. But as he eventually put the phone down, Tancred thought miserably, Of course she knows, she heard the admission in my voice as surely as I heard the knowledge in hers. After all, she's been through it enough times. What a bastard I am! But underlying daffodils were over by the end of the first week in April the

it all he felt anger at Kathie, anger because she was innocent. He
padded back into his improvised bedroom to Sushila, hitching
the towel round his waist as he went.

Sushila Nayyer had covered herself with a sheet and reclined
on his bed in the simple grandeur of her being. Sushila was now
almost nineteen, a mature and strong-minded woman. She had
stayed with Tancred and Kathie in England three years ago,
when she was studying medicine at Guy's Hospital; he had
draws in the comfort of her latest breath all dazzled with the
conceived a violent desire to sleep with her then. When his
period of UN service brought him the chance of going to
famine-struck regions of India, he had at once set about tracking Sushila down, which accounted for his presence in this
dusty camp. He still could only marvel at his luck.

'Was it your wife?' she asked. 'Phoning all the way from
I don't think you often enjoy the luxury of hearing the real
England?'

'Yes. Kathie. She was worrying about me. She always worries.
It's all right.'

They looked at each other. He wondered just how much their
inner selves understood from that glance.

'Do you want to come back on the bed with me?'

'You bet I do!'

She gave him her slow serious smile which never failed to
disturb him.

As he took off the towel, so she turned back the sheet. Because
she was a modest Muslim woman, the gesture was curiously
modest, a confidence between them. Her body, the flesh built on
O Babi Babi will the children remember me their mother like
to fine Asiatic bones, was an oasis compared with the deserts of
starved bodies outside, the famine-clad mothers who walked a
hundred miles to find water for their children. Tancred tried to
and in the well only a smell of old bones the rotted carcases of
dismiss the tiresome voices and images that punctuated his being, and climbed beside that beautiful creature, prepared even
before he touched her to possess her again. Kissing her belly, he
whose sorrows lay more siege unto my soul that all my some-
could almost ignore his disruptive and fragmentary thoughts.

37

As he buried his face in her strange-smelling black hair, the phone convulsed itself into life again.

'Sod it!' he said.

monsoon's breaking at last according to the weather station

This time, the interruption was more permanent. When he had put the phone down, he went back to Suṣhila.

'Sorry, lover-girl! I'll have to get dressed. That was Frank Young. There's an emergency call out. Bad floods at Bhagapur, and HQ want as much help as we can give. I have to go and see Young. Where the hell is Bhagapur, anyway?'

He was glad to see she was going to take this interruption without one of her displays of temper; there was only a slight trace of sulkiness in her voice as she said, 'It's a small town about fifty miles north of here, towards the Nepal border. They always have floods at Bhagapur! Will you have to go?'

Oh I don't blame you you couldn't be faithful however hard

'I hope not. It depends on Young. He says he is going with an aid unit as soon as possible.'

'It's always "as soon as possible" with that idiot Young! He is so British. Bhagapur can surely wait.'

'Postponement is an Indian virtue. In Europe, it's an admission of failure.'

He kissed her.

Dressing, Frazer went through the office and out into the road outside. As he lost the protection of the air-conditioning, he felt the monstrous heat of the plains engulf him. But the air-conditioning system had three vents, one on either side of the office block and one at the front, and it was possible to stand in the road so that one took advantage of the cooler air voided from the ugly front grill above the office door. Even so, he felt strangely ill, as he often did when standing here looking at the desolation about him.

The detachment had fenced itself off from the rest of the world; its several acres were surrounded by barbed wire. The hospital was the only considerable building in the encampment: a big square grey building down the road, already full to overflowing. All about it stood the wretched bivouacs of the refugees, a sagging village of bamboo poles and tattered sacking and plastic sheets.

The office block was nearer the gate. It was a new building, already showing signs of decay. Next to it, a new storehouse had just been completed and was already having to be repaired – part of the wall looking on to the office block had collapsed.

Although this was the stifling afternoon hour when most

to stare out through the window at the blackness of the garden

people except adulterers rested, building women were at work repairing the wall, walking slowly with dignity, bare feet grey, loads of home-made bricks in baskets on their heads, up and down the scaffolding, hardly speaking, a fold of their saris over their heads as a marginal protection against the heat.

The road straggled in front of office block and store. On the other side of the road were the old lath-built warehouse, several times robbed and now almost empty, and the light huts used as living quarters by the UN medical team. Nearer the gate were the transport section, the guard house, and other offices. That was all. A poor little punctuation on the vast monotony of the plain.

Although Frazer took all this in, for he never lost his horrified fascination with the harshness of the view and the sight of the famine victims, some of whom now squatted or stood, as he did, outside the offices, his gaze was drawn chiefly to the sky.

Towards the north, the plain died in purple haze. Above the haze, stormy rain clouds piled into the atmosphere, distorted,

you see passion and violence are a very integral part of the

compressed, angry, here black, there brilliant, as if atomic fires stirred within them. There rode the monsoon, bringing blessed rain. It looked as if it was going to fall on Chandanagar: but so it had looked for the last five nights. Instead, the rain had fallen to the north; while the wells in Chandanagar offered only a smell of old bones as the ground rotted in the three-year-old

in the well only a smell of old bones as the rotted carcass of the

drought, the river above Bhagapur flooded and washed away the inhabitants.

In my pot only broken crumbs of water only broken crumbs

An old woman called to him, extending an arm like an old broken umbrella. He crossed to Young's hut.

Frank Young was already on the move. He was in his sixties, a slaggy choleric man with sparse hair covering his skull, as heavy-jowled as he was heavy-buttocked, but still a swift-moving man when action was required of him. He had brought this UNFAW detachment into being, seen it through numerous crises, including a cholera scare, and showed no sign of giving up yet. Equally, he showed little inclination to like Frazer, although his position of command inhibited him from making it too plain. His two under-officers, Garry Knowles and Dr. Kis-

You had your orders you had no damned business leaving the

ari Mafatlal, a plump Bengali, were with him. Knowles was moving out, saying, 'I'll get the hovers ready,' as Frazer entered.

Mafatlal gave Frazer an uneasy smile. He had thick well-oiled hair and beautiful manners, both of which attributes made him appear out of place beside Frank Young. 'I was trying to explain to Mr. Young what an unpredictable river our Ganges is, and always has been throughout the entire historical times, with one branch simply entirely dry while another branch may be —'

'Yes, never mind that now, Mafatlal,' Young said brusquely. He treated the long-winded little man as a figure of fun; under Young's influence, most of the other doctors did likewise. 'Frazer, you have the picture? Severe floods in the Bhagapur area. Galbraith at HQ has just radioed me asking for full support. Over a thousand believed drowned in Bhagapur itself, and a severe landslide threatening villages a few miles from Bhagapur. I'm going to take both hovercraft and all UNFAW personnel over there, except for the hospital staff and Mafatlal. Mafatlal and you will be in charge here. We'll radio you when we get to the other end. Okay?'

'I can hardly officially take charge, sir. I'm only a visitor here. If I came with you and Knowles —'

'I want Knowles with me. Garry knows this kind of work. You sit here and hold Mafatlal's hand – and that woman doctor's, of course, Miss Nayyer. It's all routine. Just remember we have valuable stocks of grain in the new store, and keep the guards up to their duties.'

'How long do you plan to be gone?'

Controlling his exasperation, Young drew tight the straps on his sleeping bag, which he then slipped into his pocket, and said, 'That depends on the monsoon, not me, doesn't it? Damned silly question to ask, Frazer, if you don't mind my saying so.'

'Just now, I am telling Mr. Young that we may also have the flooding here also within twenty-four hours —' Mafatlal said, but Young nodded curtly and ushered them out of the room.

'Pleasant fellow,' Frazer commented sarcastically, as he stood outside with Mafatlal and watched Young's baggy figure move among the huts, calling to the other members of the team.

'Yes, he is a very pleasant fellow at heart,' said Mafatlal. 'First, you have to see into his heart. Also, his heart responds to action and then he likes to assume a very authoritarian pattern of behaviour, perhaps ingested mentally from his father at some early age – I believe his father was a military man. Don't you find, Mr. Frazer, that on the whole the man of action is an easier psychological type to get along with in everyday pursuits?'

'I never considered it.' Christ, was he going to have to listen you try to hide that you are unsure of your own psychological to Mafat's philosophizing all the while the others were gone?

'You are a man who considers more than he cares to reveal, Mr. Frazer, are you not?'

Frazer screwed up his eyes and stared at Mafatlal. Perhaps he the flower shall die and the seed but some flowers never die should confide in the doctor, tell him about the voices; sometimes they seemed oddly precognitive; as if they might be more than the signs of an inner sickness.

'I'm worried, Kisari, to tell you the truth. I just don't want to go into the matter.'

'Of course, I understand. It's good of you to tell me. But maybe I can be of more help to you than you think, because I my child child my child this poor old sack that is thy mother have always made it my business —'

'I don't want to go into it now.' He wanted to function well here, make himself useful. A little knot of refugees was closing in on him and Mafatlal. They were each given a bowl of rice gruel with vitamins every day; it was sufficient to keep them living but not properly alive. Their eyes were a torment to him. They sensed already that crisis stirred in the camp and feared it might threaten their shadowy existence. They were talking earnestly to Mafatlal in supplication; he was answering them curtly, to stare out through the window at the blackness of the as if he also had temporarily become the man of action. Between the well-fed and the starving was drawn the most rigid line of all.

Sushila appeared at the door of the office block, dressed in her neat authoritative dress. Glad to see her, Frazer crossed to her side and explained the situation.

'The people tell me that the rain will break here this evening,' she said quietly. 'If it does, the fit ones will attempt to go back

Divine Zenocrate fair is too foul an epithet for thee that in

to their villages to see if the wells have water again. Shall you let them go?'

'We do not want to stop them. There's plenty of rice and flour in the new store, but we don't know when fresh supplies will arrive, so the fewer mouths to feed here the better.'

'But you will shut the camp tonight and double the guard?'

'Yes. But there can be no danger, surely?'

'Already in Allahabad they will know this camp is almost empty of UN personnel. There are unscrupulous people about during bad times.'

He smiled. 'You are so splendidly beautiful, my divine Zenocrate! But you are over-anxious. How about getting back to the hospital to see that nobody gets jittery down there? I'll come and collect you for a drink at sundown.'

They looked at each other. He was aware that a slight breeze stirred about them. She appeared reassured by what he said, and smiled slightly.

'Perhaps if things go well I will take you on a little expedition tomorrow, Tancred,' she said. 'If you are a good boy.' She turned and walked in the direction of the hospital.

The two big hovercraft were revving their engines; dust eddied about their grey flanks. It streamed down past the women

my dust loud with the living dust singing like flies dear Siva

now lethargically ceasing the day's work on their wall, blowing away towards the hospital and the ragged encampment. It streamed past the ten men of the UNFAW team as, packs on backs, they moved towards the air-cushion vehicles. They waved a salutation to Frazer and Mafatlal as they went.

try to get back before my birthday Tancred you know it

Frazer and Mafatlal stood in the roadway until the machines

moved off. They watched as they moved slowly across the stricken plain, two whirling pillars of dust blowing with them. By that time, the building women had climbed down from their wooden scaffolding and were trailing back towards their quarters. But the refugees still sat or lay listlessly in the shade, or stood where the grill of the inefficient air-conditioner poured a cooler wind out of the office block.

In the sky, the granite clouds puffed and flattened themselves, *the roses need the rain although it's lovely to have the spell of denying rain*. Cold and desolation took hold of Frazer; he *es liegt der heisse Sommer* while in my heart the winter is lying thought with melancholy of his betrayed wife. I can't damned help it, Kathie; I'm a victim of lust or something – maybe I never had enough breast-feeding as an infant. Probably Mafat could explain it to me....

He did not need explanations but he needed a drink. Desiring company, he asked Mafatlal in for one as well.

The little doctor would have only a small whisky, well-diluted, and with sugar in. He admitted he preferred it diluted with champagne, but only water was available. As he toyed with the drink, he made polite conversation, to which Frazer gave random answers. Finally, he said, 'Mr. Frazer, may I make a personal statement?'

'Go ahead.'

'I am always wondering why I find it very difficult to strike up a confidence with English and American men. Would you say that that might be because of certain possibly faulty qualities in my own character which repel them?'

'God, I don't know, Kisari! Speaking for myself, I find all these personal questions pretty embarrassing, and so do a lot of people.'

'Ah, but should you find them embarrassing? Should there not be fewer barriers between people? Perhaps the old saying is true that Englishmen are reserved and want only to live within themselves.'

Slightly irritated, Frazer said, 'Actually, I am not English at all. I am Swiss. It just happens I've lived in England most of my life, and my wife is English.'

Mafatlal put his head on one side inquiringly. 'I see! Well, I

would not say that that invalidates my thesis. You may have
picked up the habit of shutting yourself away from your fellow
men and so you can perhaps talk only to women, isn't it?'

Frazer got up and poured himself another whisky. Disturbed
by it though he was, he could not help seeing the funny side of
this interview.

if you are a good boy I will take you on a little expedition to—

'Kisari, I know you have a degree in psychoanalysis. Why not
turn it against yourself? You really want to talk to me about
Sushila, don't you? You're just eaten up with jealousy because
you think I'm lying with her every day, aren't you?'

'Any man might envy you the body of Sushila Nayyer,
Tancred, indeed, yes! – Though I have other fish to cook with
my lady loves of the hospital nursing staff. But I know why you
feel so guilty about your enjoyment of Sushila.'

'Guilty! I do not feel guilty! It's not a question – look, as
I've said before, I find these personal discussions very unpleasant indeed. If you have finished your drink, perhaps you
wouldn't mind leaving me in peace, damn it!'

Mafatlal set down his glass and gestured sadly. 'May I say
may I say that you ease your conscience by confessing to your
that you would be better perhaps if you also took the sugar
lump in your whisky? Totally no offence, of course. Life is sour
enough for all of us. . . .'

He stood up, for once leaving a sentence unfinished. Nodding, he walked out of Frazer's temporary apartment, through
the office, and out into the road. Very dignified, Frazer thought.
Very dignified, if a pain in the neck. He did not feel guilty
the habit of shutting yourself away from your fellow men and
about Sushila. Well, not in the way Mafatlal meant. But it
might have been worth hearing what the long-winded little
blighter had to say on the subject. . . . Mafatlal was no fool;
Sushila thought highly of him.

He sat down and drained his glass, suddenly miserable.
Dusk was sweeping in. Once more rain was not coming to Chandanagar this evening. No doubt it was plastering down on
Bhagapur instead. He genuinely sorrowed for the wretched
famine victims; at the same time, the sight of all that malnutrition, all those starving children, filled him with so much

44

unease that he could hardly tolerate the possibility of any more refugees. Often it seemed to be their voices that he heard in his head. Anxiously he thought, it's a deep spiritual sickness from which I suffer. My stomach churns all the time. And the air-conditioning plant growled at him.

a lover and his beloved came together in the evening when

As the night gathered, he went out to collect Sushila from the hospital. A family was admitted through the main gate just before it closed for the night. The man stalked in front, white-haired, hollow-eyed, carrying a child; his wife walked behind him, an iron cooking pot on her head and two boys tagging beside her. An older girl followed them; she also carried a child. All the children seemed near death; the boys mere walking skeletons, every rib showing; the girl like a little old woman. Their skins were furry with dust. An orderly, a plump Bihari girl with a diamond glinting at one nostril, led them down towards the kitchens.

Frazer followed the group slowly. Now, at the dawn of the twenty-first century, most of the world was eating factory-made foods, and enjoying them. In India, people refused to touch them, just as they still refused fish. During the nineteen-eighties, events had taken a progressive turn, and a contraceptive pill had at last gone some way towards being accepted; then had come the big Bombay Chemicals scandal, when over two thousand women had died from a wrongly made-up consignment of the pills. Adverse publicity had set everything back once more. There had followed a religiously-inspired revolt against the Climate-Control Board which, while it always had to rob Peter to pay Paul, had at least gone some way to eliminate droughts. Now the sub-continent was sliding back to the perilous political and economic situation that had beset it back in the fifties and sixties. Currently, the standard of living was higher in the equatorial belt of Mars than it was in Uttar Pradesh.

All about the hospital, where the disgraced bivouacs clustered and the daffodils were almost over by the end of the first week in the failing light, spirals of smoke drifted up from glowing *sigris* and oil lamps gleamed here and there. No breeze stirred now. Again the monsoon had turned its back on this section of the pitiless plain. On this further night, the orgy of the living and the dying could take place undisturbed by hope.

that's it rub it against me darling your fabulous briney juices

Frazer spent next morning industriously touring and inspecting the camp. All was in order, as far as order went. Nobody was dying; everyone was getting a statistically-decided minimum quota of calories. If there was no real famine in camp, equally there was no infectious disease. What there was was suffering, the long attrition of semi-starvation which brought stupidity and indifference and welcomed in any number of physical defects. Frazer believed in the body; it was one of the few things you could trust; he hated to see this large-scale wastage of it. Especially he hated to see cadaverous women bringing forth babies and nestling them to dry dugs. It was a travesty of the life process.

Beyond the camp perimeter stretched baked land with patches of scrub standing out vaguely, like the discoloured patches on the skin of a tertiary syphilitic. Here and there, he could see cattle tottering about the *maidan*; some had followed trails to Chandanagar, hoping for water. The beasts were hollow and rotten. One fell over sideways even as Frazer looked. The vultures who sat about the camp moved over to its carcass, walking slowly across the ground like shabby Calcutta clerks with their hands behind their backs. They never flew in the Chandanagar area unless you ran up and tried to kick them, as *the stinking bastards pull the guts out of the ass first of all and* Frazer sometimes did; death could be tackled at walking-pace in Uttar Pradesh.

Delhi has had enough sir Delhi is tired of other people's

'I've had enough of this place,' Frazer said to Sushila over lunch. He was eating in the cool hospital-staff dining-room, taking a fresh lime juice and gin with his artificial rump steak. 'Can't we get out of here and drive into Faizabad for the evening? Young just radioed that they're going to be away all week, as far as he can see.'

'Whom will you leave in charge?'

'Kisari Mafatlal, of course. He's senior to me.'

You're eaten up with jealousy because you think I'm lying

With her magnetic eyes fixed on his, she said, 'The people will be very distressed to see you go; you know that, don't you,

Tancred?'

'Oh, what nonsense!' But he was conscious of a slight feeling
and from the love we've built let's go out and love and help
of guilt. 'They care nothing about me. They're too busy with
their own preoccupations, to be interested in anything I do.'

'That is not so. However, if you are happy....' Her beautiful
voice, long remembered in cool rooms.

'I am happy. The bright lights and madding crowds of Faizabad, then?'

'Darling, you forget I told you yesterday I have a little expedition to take you on.'

'No. Oh, yes, of course! Have I been a good boy? Where do
we go?' He felt the sickness again as she began her explanation.
He wanted to get out of camp; but when the chance came to go,
he could think only of the heat and the death waiting outside.

There was no trouble about their commandeering a truck. As
Frazer walked over to the offices, wretched groups of refugees
still waited where the cool air gushed out on them, the labouring women still moved in a dream-time up and down their
scaffolding. He left word with a *chuprassi* to tell Mafatlal where
he was going.
a very pleasant fellow at heart but his heart responds to action

Sushila was wearing a short stiff skirt which contrasted
piquantly with a white blouse buttoning high on her neck; it
lent her a misleading air of primness. She took the seat beside
Frazer, gave him directions as they rolled out of the main gate
and leaned back to light a cigar when he switched the truck on
to automatic.

'I'm taking you to see my parents' house, Tancred. I thought
that would be very pleasant for you. There are some clothes I
wish to collect. I have nothing to wear in camp.'

'I thought you had quarrelled with your father.'

'My father is not at home. He has moved to the hills where
there is no drought. There is only an old family *chokidar* guarding the house. He has been instructed not to admit me, but he
will because he loves me.'

'*Shabash!* Sounds like a great homecoming!'

'Anyhow, it's a lovely afternoon for a drive, darling.'

'Oh, yes, bloody great! Lovely scenery, too!'

'You will be fond of it when you grow used to it.'

He felt uneasy and irritable. An emotion was coming from her which he could not analyse; of recent months, he had become so confident of interpreting what other people were feeling that to be baffled worried him unduly.

They were now entering the land of the dead, where the only colour was the colour of cow dung. The camp had fallen behind and was swallowed into heat haze. The rutted track they followed led from nowhere into nowhere under the gilt dome of sky, never deviating even when they passed through villages. *from another century this enormous lugubrious hotel deserted* The villages stood petrifying, without motion, moribund, as if *and I only an old cup of clay that fills only with the bitter heat* time had turned to jelly in the wrath of the sun. Occasionally, a *how can you be starved for sex I give you all I've got don't I in* paper-thin cow stood arrested in a doorway, occasionally a mangy dog ran from the truck, occasionally an old man or woman died at their leisure in a patch of shade. The beaks of *you've always been sheltered what do you know of suffering or* well-arms pointed up to the sky. Desolation seemed less tyran- *privileged idle life shut away from knowledge of the real* nous outside the villages.

Gradually, habitation grew more frequent. The road became increasingly broken, turning downhill in uneasy rushes. It emerged on a river bank.

This was one of the many streams of the Ganges. Distantly, water could be seen, bracketed between miles of sand and dried mud. Dirty shacks had been built on the mud flats, life had been contrived; suddenly one evening would come the foaming floods and sweep that pitiful contrivance away – it could be tonight.

They drove along the track that followed the river bank. Flies buzzed in the cab with them. A few coarse trees grew here, desiccated and grey; only palm trees flourished in the drought. Vultures and kite hawks sat in cindery bushes, meditative. A scarecrow stalked along the road, burdened under a dripping water-skin. He walked on for several minutes before Frazer's hooting dislodged him from the crown of the road.

48

'Silly old sod! Where is this house of yours, anyway? How much further do we have to go through this god-blasted desert?'

She pointed ahead. 'Behind those trees there.' Leaning forward eagerly, she threw her cigar butt out of the window.

The Nayyer family house was walled round with white walls and guarded with huge wooden gates. Through cracks in the timber, they spied an aged Sikh, snoozing on a *charpoy* in the shade of a wizened mango tree. By dint of much calling and whistling, he was roused and eventually let them through the gate, grumbling to himself at the nuisance of it all.

The house was large, girt with verandas and balconies, smothered with dying vine. It had been pretty in better days. To one side, overlooked by giant pines, lay a cracked brown area where a pleasant pool had once lain. A *chokidar* in a faded green tunic appeared, making *salaam* to Sushila.

He let them in a side door, an old grey unshaven man in slippers, chewing *betel*. All doors and shutters in the house were tightly closed. A scent hung in the corridors which seemed compounded of the world's nostalgia, flowers and dust and where forgotten things belong you keep coming back like a wood smoke and the dross of human lives.

the daffodils will be out when you return and we'll still be the

She left him to wander round as she went up to her old room. The *chokidar* brought a warm bottled grapefruit juice for Frazer to drink; he walked about, sipping at the tumbler, curious to see everything. The furniture was heavy and dark; secrets were wardrobed into every shadowy room; the house waited. Frazer experienced a strong sense of intrusion, and of excitement. Suddenly, he wanted Sushila and hurried up the wide stone stairs to find her.

Sushila was in her bedroom; she had opened one shutter, so that an angle of sun burned into the room by the window, lighting everything by reflection. She was bending over a trunk, pulling out lengths of sari. When Frazer entered she turned, her you dirty swine you're at her all the time aren't you won't face lit from below, seeing instantly what he wanted.

She twiddled fingers on a level with her ear, in a gesture of disapproval. Who else could frown and smile at the same time?

'No, Tancred, no sex! We ought to get back. Now that we're here, I'm anxious to get back to the camp, in case there is trouble there.' She slammed down the trunk lid.

'To hell with camp! I want you here in your own surroundings, not in a concentration camp!' He grasped her fiercely, thrusting one hand round her shoulders and the other between her legs, pulling her, fighting with her to get her on to the bed, _the rosy glow of summer is on thy dimpled cheek awhile in thy_ She always responded to violence, wonderful girl, strong as a _while in thy heart the winter is lying cold and bleak es liegt der_ panther considering how fragile she was, spirited, savage, the savage always there ready to wake again. . . .

They fell on to the bed, raising a cloud of dust. She was slapping him about the neck, cursing him.

'Oh, you sod, you dirty Swiss sod, you lecherous dirty Swiss sod!'

'Let us, you bitch, _dekko chute!_'

you're like all the Europeans you're just a spoiler I can't

On the white counterpane under the drapes of muslin mosquito net, they struggled, he dragging and tearing at her clothes until, bit by bit, her body was revealed. She was still struggling – with him now, not against.

Now walk the angels on the walls of heaven as sentinels to

It was quick and brutal for him, soon over.

Afterwards, she was furious again. She marched up and down the room as he lay on the bed, grabbing up her torn clothes and cursing him, damning him for ruining her possessions.

'Go back to camp in a sari, then! You've got a mass of them here!'

'You bloody Europeans, you're all the same! You're just a spoiler, spoil this, spoil that, spoil everything, don't care! Oh, I warn you, honestly, Tancred, I hate you, I hate you so stinking much, you rapist swine, I just can't tell you possibly! You have no standards!'

He had already heard her say it all in his head. He was sick with precognition, ashamed of himself, disgusted with her.

Suddenly, she flung a brass vase at Frazer. It struck the wall above him and bounced away. He jumped off the bed and grabbed her wrist, squeezing it until she sank to the floor, gasping with pain.

'Don't you fling things at me, you little wild cat! Put a sari on, and let's be getting back to camp! *Jaldhi jao!*'

stocks of grain and remember to keep the guards up to their

She selected a magnificent twelve-yard sari, all copper and brown and crimson, and wound it slowly about her body, saying, 'I will never lie with you again; I prefer fat Kisari Mafatlal to you. You are so common! You have a wife at home, you common man! Wouldn't you be ashamed if she knew you were going with a coloured woman?'

He put his shoes on and went over to the balcony, looking out over the dying garden. A parakeet with red head and green wings swooped down on to a lower veranda. It landed almost at the feet of an old woman standing actionless at the veranda rail, only to dart off again immediately. Perhaps the old woman was the *chokidar*'s wife. Frazer was happy to think that she probably did not understand English. When she looked up at him, he retired into the bedroom. Sushila was arranging her hair, her brows heavy, all full of honey, superb.

so shall the flower die and the seed and some flowers shall

'You're beautiful, Sushila. I know I'm a bastard but I love you!'

'You do not love me! And I know why you want me, because Mafatlal told me.'

'Never mind Mafatlal. Let's get on! The sky's clouding up. If the monsoon struck now, we'd be stuck here.'

Her hand flew to her mouth. 'Oh, my confounded Christ! Then there'd be real trouble! Us marooned here and Young coming back to Chandanagar and finding you'd cleared off and stolen his best lady doctor and left his flock unguarded.'

Her words made him angrier. The bitch was getting at him! He marched downstairs and into the garden, revving the truck impatiently as she stayed on the terrace to talk to the *chokidar*, who was now joined by the old woman Frazer had seen from the window. This old woman carried Sushila's suitcaseful of belongings and placed it reverently in the back of the truck. Sush-

while in my heart the winter is lying cold and bleak and the

ila waved to the old couple as the truck began to roll.

As they drove along by the shrunken river's bank, he sang an old song of Heine's which his mother had taught him long ago, back in the Lauterbrunnen days: *'Es liegt der heisse Sommer'*, keeping it going as they roared through the fossilized villages.

His head ached. Finally he said, 'I'm giving up, Sushila. India's not for me. I'm going back home as soon as possible. I'm no good out here – I haven't the dedication the job requires.'

She was still angry and said nothing. To draw her out, to flatter her, he said, 'Your country is too harsh for me, Sushila. You survive in it, fragile as a flower, but it's killing me. I've felt ill ever since I came to Chandanagar. Perhaps you're right and I'm a common man.'

you are so common wouldn't you be ashamed if she knew you

Adamant, she said, 'You're a spoiler, Tancred, like all your race. You make me feel dirty. That's all I have to say to you.'

'That's all, eh? No deep Indian wisdom to give to the disappearing white man! There's a myth in Switzerland – and in England too – that India is a land of ancient wisdom, where eventually a man will come face to face with the knowledge of himself. Have you nothing like that to offer, eh, instead of catty remarks?'

She laughed. 'You often come face to face with yourself, Tancred, but you will not acknowledge it.'

'Tell me, then! Give me a piece of your wisdom, the immemorial wisdom of the East! What does go on inside that brain of yours, anyway, sex apart?'

She began to light a cigar, and only then looked at him through the smoke.

'I will tell you! I will tell you something to keep stored among the funny voices in your head. Perhaps you will strike me, but I don't care! I don't think you often get the luxury of hearing the real truth about yourself, do you? You have come to Chandanagar and the famine because it represents a state of

Mutti Mutti I didn't mean it really I didn't mean it don't cry

mind to you from your childhood. I don't know what. And there you have come to me to torment me because I also represent to you something other than what I really am. You see, you cannot understand famine as famine, because it is a thing alien to your part of the world, and so for you it can be believed only as a famine of love. That you can experience! It is the common experience of Europe and America, the famine of love. Your lands are deserts in that sense. Your famine of love is your big neurosis that drives you to live among machinery.'

'You're joking, of course!' He laughed harshly.

She arched her superb eyebrows and did not smile.

'And you suffer the malnutrition of the soul, which brings all kinds of shadow-diseases to you. You have been pushed to seek comfort in my bosom because you have to respond in that way to the hunger all round you, as the psychic forces of Chandanagar bear down on you. But even to my bosom you have to bring your deeper discontents from other times. Even my bosom you make your battleground! Your dirty common adulterous battleground! You are slowly dying, even as the people in the UNFAW enclosure.'

He had not expected to hear it, rattling in the truck with death's landscape leaden under the storm clouds. Her words were a terrible torment for him; no precognition prepared him for her judgement. It took away his defences of anger, so that their relationship was at an end, that she had killed it as deliberately as one chops off a snake's head. He wished he could have wept.

She spoke again as the vehicle turned away from the river.

'My wisdom comes mostly not from me, but from Kisari Mafatlal. He understands about all the matters people do not you try to hide that you are unsure of your own psychological care to reveal. I believe he knows what you are really like underneath.'

'Do you have to discuss me with him?'

'Don't sound so much like an old beaten dog! When we spoke of you, we hoped only that we could help find yourself.'

'Very good of you to put yourself out on my account!' The withering sarcasm withered and died. Mafatlal, that windbag, talking seriously with, sharing confidences with, Sushila! It might be wondered what else they shared! These Indians, they were so treacherous.... Even a girl educated in England....
the tulips were over by the end of the last week in April with You never knew.

The long afternoon was tiring visibly over the immense bowl of plain when they sighted the camp. Neither spoke to the other as the truck bumped forward over the last mile. Again the monsoon clouds were gigantic in the sky although not a drop of moisture spilled from their purple lips.

She said, 'The gate's shut already!'

He peered ahead, instinctively accelerating the truck.

The gate was indeed closed. Flipping off the automatics, he steered the truck until its nose was thrust hard against the wire-shielded pole now barring the gateway. He jumped out, shouting in Hindi as he did so for the guards to lift the barrier.

Two men ran forward, very black and in filthy clothes. Frazer had never seen them before. Both were armed. They fired at him. As he flung himself down, he heard the windshield shatter behind him and a bullet go screaming into space. Diving behind the truck, he climbed up and fumbled in the tool box for a weapon. There was not enough time: the men were on him. Frazer flung himself at one of them, but the man whippd up his rifle, so that Frazer ran against it. The other man clamped his weapon round Frazer's throat.

'Don't make struggle, *sahib*!'

He had little chance of struggling. They had him tight. Neither looked the kind who would mind killing him. Another man ran up, shouting. He hauled Sushila out of the front of the truck; she stood unconcernedly brushing shattered glass off her sari. As she and Frazer were led past the guard house, he saw the guards lined up against a wall inside, their palms to the wall and their trousers down, as a bandit with a rifle stood over them. The camp had undergone a change of ownership, it seemed.

'This is all your fault, Frazer!' Sushila said.

Two strange trucks were inside the camp. One stood outside the new store, one was further down, covering the hospital.

He knew what the raiders were after, of course. The grain! The store was full of rice, plus large quantities of wheat and flour, as well as canned goods. Plundering would start any moment.

The bandits marched him and Sushila roughly down the road. They stopped by the store, the doors of which were closed, and one of them shouted something, evidently to a superior inside. The store door opened and a ferocious face peered out. It belonged to a large Indian with a thatch of lank hair. He was the very glow of summer is on thy dimpled cheek cold and eating. In an angry-sounding exchange, he gestured to the office block next door, and threw Frazer's captor a key.

Frazer and Sushila were then dragged to the offices. The door was unlocked, and their captors told them to stay inside and we always keep all the shutters closed when we're away to keep quiet, adding that they were lucky to escape so lightly. They were pushed in and the door slammed and locked on them.

'Oh God, they are robbing the store!' Frazer said.

Sushila strolled over to a swivel chair and sat down, resting her delicate wrists on the desk.

'They will make sure they get a good feed first! The bosses sit in the store having a feast while the underlings keep watch outside! They will have cut all communications with the outside world. There is nothing we can do! They are desperate! They will take everything!'

To his surprise, she began to wail with her face in her hands. Frazer began pacing about.

'What a fool I was to leave camp! ... But even if the bandits have rounded up the doctors at the hospital, won't the refugees do something to save the food stocks?'

'What can those poor people do? When *can* they do? They will do nothing.'

Of course it was true. It was the history of India. Some of the refugees had even been standing about outside, waiting in the cool used air ejected from this building, as if nothing was happening that could possibly concern them.

A frightened clerk appeared on the stairs. The bandits had shut the clerks in the office block too, under pain of instant death if they attempted to get out.

Frazer followed him back upstairs, suddenly hopeful.

'We'll barge the door down! How many of you are there? We can rush the bandits while the pigs are still eating.'

There were ten clerks upstairs. Shame-faced, they revealed why they would not venture out of the building: the bandits had a napalm gun. They were threatening the hospital with it at the moment, but they would turn it on anyone who made any trouble.

Frazer went downstairs again and explained to the girl about the napalm gun. She stared ahead, saying nothing.

'That's why they are so confident! Sushila, we *must* do some-
you had your orders Frazer you had no business deserting the
thing! I'm not just going to wait here while they fill their stomachs!'

Furious and frustrated, he ran into the room he used as a bedroom. Kisari Mafatlal lay on his camp bed, a clerk tending him and bathing his forehead. The plump little doctor had been badly beaten about the face; he peered at Frazer out of an enormously puffed eye. The latter called Sushila in.

Through painful lips, Mafatlal told Frazer and Sushila how the bandits had arrived at the gate in their two trucks, claiming to be bringing stores from Allahabad. The gate guard, not expecting stores, had been suspicious and called Mafatlal. Mafatlal had been wary enough to ring through to UNFAW HQ and warn them that, if he did not phone again in five minutes, it would mean trouble at the camp. Then he had gone bravely to the gate, asked to see the stores that the bandits claimed they were bringing, and had been clobbered.

'How long ago was this?'

'It only just happened, as you can see. I was thrown in here to die!'

'Thank God the HQ police will soon be along!'

'It will take them one hour at the earliest to arrive here. Then these pigs will all be escaped across the *maidan*.'

you had your orders Frazer and I hold you entirely responsible

'There must be something we can do! Sushila, look after Kisari; I'm going to scout round.'

He needed – he did not know what. He unlocked the door into the basement and hurried down the crude concrete steps, seeking a weapon. The self-powered air-conditioning plant was here, labouring away, its semi-audible note creating a pain in
your deeper discontents from other times even my bosom you
the teeth, as always. Apart from the plant, the cellar was bare.
shadow-diseases even my bosom by the first week of April
He skirted it, prepared to go, stopped.

Stuffing his handkerchief into his mouth to hinder the vibrations, he rolled an empty oil drum over to one wall, rammed it there with a brick, and climbed on to it. The voices in his head tormented him.

By pushing aside the clumsy metal ventilator that spewed out used air, he could look through the grill on to the store where to stare again out through the window at the blackness of the the bandits were feasting. The wooden scaffolding was in place, will the little ones remember me their mother an old withered although the women labouring to repair the wall had been sent no milk but dust and in my bowl only these broken grains of away. Even the new wall showed cracks. The wall round the tender mouths tender mouths you are slowly dying tender ventilator grill against which Frazer stood was also a maze of cracks.

'All that vibration...' he muttered. He was trembling, almost all that vibration April is the cruellest month bringing Christ delirious.

As he checked over the unwieldy machine, throbbing to itself, memories stirred in him. The plant was a primitive machine, with the legend 'Made in Bombay' and a patent number and the date '1979' proudly displayed on its flank. Over twenty years old! But of course, it wasn't the vibration as such....

Hastily, he followed the circuit through the refrigeration plant, saw the air ducts snake out through the cavity walling. It would be possible to switch off most of the circuit, and concentrate the output of the machine through the one grill.... Suddenly, he knew what he wanted, and was running back upstairs to Sushila.

'Sushila, help me lift Kisari enough to get the blankets from under him. I need the blankets. Then ... that's it! ... then, I want to borrow your sari....'

Before she could flare up, he explained his plan. As he spoke, she watched his mouth with suspicion and contempt.

In the end, she shrugged and unwound the flaring material from her body until she stood there in brassiere and panties. Gratefully, he passed her a clean shirt from his trunk. With her help, he swathed himself in the blankets, and she bound them to him and over his head with the sari. She did then smile at him, and he grinned back.

When he was completely muffled from head to foot, he fumbled his way downstairs again.

He switched off power, then went round ripping out connections. Soon, the giant ventilator would concentrate all its output through the one ventilator overlooking the new store.

Gritting his teeth, Frazer switched on again.

He could hear very little now. But he could feel the waves of sound. He knew he was right, even as he felt his stomach quivering. This was infrasound. The plant was emitting slow air vibrations at less than ten hertz – the human ear could only register sound from sixteen hertz up. The compressions were radiating outwards, mostly in one direction only, like a primitive death-ray. Even the voices in his head were silenced.

Peering through the fringes of his blankets, and through the fine silk of the sari, Frazer looked anxiously towards the ventilator. He could hear secondary vibrations setting up in the steel grill, a low moan rising and falling, almost like the monsoon wind coming in over the plains. How long should he give it? He could not see out —

A curiously pulsating roar reached his ears. It could only be.... He dashed forward and switched off his deadly machine. The roar took on a steadier note and became identifiable as masonry falling. Panting, Frazer dragged the sari and blankets from his head, feeling as sick as a dog. Staggering over to the wall, he knocked the vent aside and looked out. Nothing could be seen for a great billowing cloud of red dust!

Calling, shouting incoherently, he made his way upstairs.

'Help me get this padding off, Sushila, and we'll go outside!' As she unwrapped him, he thought that, although the blankets had saved him from some of the vibrations, the infrasound had given his body a thorough shake-up. He was feeling brittle and cold right inside his bones; a continuous whine seemed to have set up in the coils of his intestines.

With Sushila following, dressed in his shirt and a pair of his shorts, and looking mouth-wateringly seductive, Frazer marched into the front office and hurled himself at the door. On his third charge, one of the wooden panels broke; he pushed it
you're just a spoiler spoil this spoil that spoil everything don't

away and climbed outside, helping the girl out after him.

'How did you do it?' she asked. The awe in her voice thrilled him. She grasped his hand, staring at the great reddish cloud of dust now clearing.

Through the cloud, they could see that the near wall of the store had collapsed, carrying the plastic roofing with it. The store was otherwise still more or less standing, although cracks marked the whole façade of it. The contents should not have suffered too much damage.

'I'm just a spoiler,' Frazer said. 'I spoil everything – but in this case, you might add that the spoiling had been going on for a long while. That's why they always had trouble with the wall. Our air-conditioning was permanently beaming low-power infrasound at it; all I did was step up the power.'

'I don't understand at all. You did this with sound?'

'Yes, infrasound. Sound you can't hear: slow air vibration, in fact.' He had to hold on to her shoulder to stand steady. 'It creates a sort of pendulum action, which can quickly build up a dead reverberation in solid objects or in human beings. Can't you feel your stomach and heart vibrating?'

'I feel sick, yes. It's just excitement, I think.'

'It's infrasound. Maybe infrasound is a source of emotional excitement. Maybe I owe the voices I hear in my head to the faulty air-conditioner. Ever since I've been here, I've had a low-hunger all round you as the psychic forces of Chandanagar powered death ray turned on me all the time. What you said you have been pushed to seek comfort in my bosom because was right – I was slowly dying. Literally slowly dying.'

'But you switched the machine off now?'

He nodded. 'Perhaps I shan't be such a bastard now.'

They looked at each other cautiously. To cover all that he was feeling, Frazer said, 'Let's go and see what's happened to the bandits.'

'Will they be dead?'

'I hope not.' He started shouting to the guards in the gate-house. The bandits who had been keeping the guards quiet were now standing by the front of the ruined store. With the initiative taken out of their hands, they made no attempt to stop Frazer as he went up and opened the store door.

Dust swirled out of the interior. He stepped back, choking. In a minute or two, the bandits emerged, sorry and sick, all but one crawling on hands and knees. Frazer had an idea of what they would be feeling; their invisible injuries would include an intense irritation internally, as if their various organs had been set rubbing against each other by the low-pitched sound. They would have recovered by tomorrow. And, by then, they would be in the lock-up in Allahabad. The doctors down at the hospital were already rounding up the bandits with the napalm weapon; the calamity to their leaders had robbed them of the will to fight.

Still the monsoon did not break, still the reinforcements from UNFAW HQ which Mafatlal had alerted did not arrive; perhaps the very pleasant man operating the switchboard had forgotten all about the detachment and its problems. It was a very Indian situation.

Mafatlal's wounds had been treated and he was resting in his own room. Sushila and Frazer sat by him, drinking. She wore silver sandals on her feet. Although Frazer was the hero of the hour, Mafatlal was the invalid of the hour and enjoying the situation to the full.

'You see, Tancred, passion and violence are a very integral part of the Indian scene. But they come and then they are gone, he understands about all matters people do not care to reveal as also applies to humanity. But the things they represent are always a permanency, which we must tolerate in the most philosophical way.' His gestures were exquisite. He was moved by his own words. 'The flower shall die and the seed and some flowers shall never ever die, as Krishna says, stating the paradox of life. It is, you will agree, somewhat of a rather Indian situation from your point of view, perhaps. . . .'

Frazer doubted if Sushila was listening. At the present moment, the characters of the three of them were in equipoise; but that would not last. The dynamic of the girl's life was unfolding – even in these stagnant surroundings – inevitably to work what is beauty saith my sufferings then? Divine Zenocrate, if against any stability. The remoteness of the expression on her beautiful face contradicted any sociability expressed in her clutched gin-glass.

And he.... He wondered if it might be possible to resume those happy intimacies with her. Nothing was final – in Uttar Pradesh, even finality wore a temporary aspect. Both she and

you have been pushed to seek comfort in my bosom just be-

Mafatlal were slightly in awe of him at the moment, since he had played so actively his rôle of the westerner, the spoiler; so the time might be propitious for him to try his luck with her again. Or should he wait till Young returned, face the trouble of that encounter, and then inaugurate his return to England and Kathie? He would do what he would do; what others said or thought about him could make no difference to him, could it? Right now, he would listen to Mafatlal, gaze on Sushila, and have another drink.

Tomorrow, he would decide. He would see how he felt. De-

the flower shall die and the seed and some flowers shall never

cisions could be postponed. That also was a very Indian situation.

the flower shall die and the seed and some flowers shall never

In Mrs. Swinton's garden, it was always summer. The lovely almond trees stood about it in perpetual leaf. Monica Swinton plucked a saffron-coloured rose and showed it to David.

'Isn't it lovely?' she said.

David looked up at her and grinned without replying. Seizing the flower, he ran with it across the lawn and disappeared behind the kennel where the mowervator crouched, ready to cut or sweep or roll when the moment dictated. She stood alone on her impeccable plastic gravel path.

She had tried to love him.

When she made up her mind to follow the boy, she found him in the courtyard floating the rose in his paddling pool. He stood in the pool engrossed, still wearing his sandals.

'David, darling, do you have to be so awful? Come in at once and change your shoes and socks.'

He went with her without protest into the house, his dark head bobbing at the level of her waist. At the age of three, he showed no fear of the ultra-sonic dryer in the kitchen. But before his mother could reach for a pair of slippers, he wriggled away and was gone into the silence of the house.

He would probably be looking for Teddy.

Monica Swinton, twenty-nine, of graceful shape and lambent eye, went and sat in her living-room, arranging her limbs with taste. She began by sitting and thinking; soon she was just sitting. Time waited on her shoulder with the maniac sloth it reserves for children, the insane, and wives whose husbands are away improving the world. Almost by reflex, she reached out and changed the wavelength of her windows. The garden faded; in its place, the city centre rose by her left hand, full of crowding people, blowboats, and buildings – but she kept the sound down. She remained alone. An overcrowded world is the ideal place in which to be lonely.

The directors of Synthank were eating an enormous luncheon to celebrate the launching of their new product. Some of them wore the plastic face-masks popular at the time. All were elegantly slender, despite the rich food and drink they were putting away. Their wives were elegantly slender, despite the food and drink they too were putting away. An earlier and less sophisticated generation would have regarded them as beautiful people, apart from their eyes.

Henry Swinton, Managing Director of Synthank, was about to make a speech.

'I'm sorry your wife couldn't be with us to hear you,' his neighbour said.

'Monica prefers to stay at home thinking beautiful thoughts,' said Swinton, maintaining a smile.

'One would expect such a beautiful woman to have beautiful thoughts,' said the neighbour.

Take your mind off my wife, you bastard, thought Swinton, still smiling.

He rose to make his speech amid applause.

After a couple of jokes, he said, 'Today marks a real breakthrough for the company. It is now almost ten years since we put our first synthetic life-forms on the world market. You all know what a success they have been, particularly the miniature dinosaurs. But none of them had intelligence.

'It seems like a paradox that in this day and age we can create life but not intelligence. Our first selling line, the Crosswell Tape, sells best of all, and is the most stupid of all.'

Everyone laughed.

'Though three-quarters of our overcrowded world are starving, we are lucky here to have more than enough, thanks to population control. Obesity's our problem, not malnutrition. I guess there's nobody round this table who doesn't have a Crosswell working for him in the small intestine, a perfectly safe parasite tape-worm that enables its host to eat up to 50 per cent more food and still keep his or her figure. Right?' General nods of agreement.

'Our miniature dinosaurs are almost equally stupid. Today, we launch an intelligent synthetic life-form – a full-size serving-man.

'Not only does he have intelligence, he has a controlled amount of intelligence. We believe people would be afraid of a being with a human brain. Our serving-man has a small computer in his cranium.

'There have been mechanicals on the market with mini-computers for brains – plastic things without life, super-toys – but we have at last found a way to link computer circuitry with synthetic flesh.'

David sat by the long window of his nursery, wrestling with paper and pencil. Finally, he stopped writing and began to roll the pencil up and down the slope of the desk-lid.

'Teddy!' he said.

Teddy lay on the bed against the wall, under a book with moving pictures and a giant plastic soldier. The speech-pattern of his master's voice activated him and he sat up.

'Teddy, I can't think what to say!'

Climbing off the bed, the bear walked stiffly over to cling to the boy's leg. David lifted him and set him on the desk.

'What have you said so far?'

'I've said —' He picked up his letter and stared hard at it. 'I've said, "Dear Mummy, I hope you're well just now. I love you. . . ."'

There was a long silence, until the bear said, 'That sounds fine. Go downstairs and give it to her.'

Another long silence.

'It isn't quite right. She won't understand.'

Inside the bear, a small computer worked through its programme of possibilities. 'Why not do it again in crayon?'

When David did not answer, the bear repeated his suggestion. 'Why not do it again in crayon?'

David was staring out of the window. 'Teddy, you know what I was thinking? How do you tell what are real things from what aren't real things?'

The bear shuffled its alternatives. 'Real things are good.'

'I wonder if time is good. I don't think Mummy *likes* time very much. The other day, lots of days ago, she said that time went by her. Is time real, Teddy?'

'Clocks tell the time. Clocks are real. Mummy has clocks so she must like them. She has a clock on her wrist next to her dial.'

David had started to draw a jumbo-jet on the back of his letter. 'You and I are real, Teddy, aren't we?'

The bear's eyes regarded the boy unflinchingly. 'You and I are real, David.' It specialized in comfort.

Monica walked slowly about the house. It was almost time for the afternoon post to come over the wire. She punched the GPO number on the dial on her wrist but nothing came through. A few minutes more.

She could take up her painting. Or she could dial her friends. Or she could wait till Henry came home. Or she could go up and play with David. . . .

She walked out into the hall and to the bottom of the stairs. 'David!'

No answer. She called again and a third time.

'Teddy!' she called, in sharper tones.

'Yes, Mummy!' After a moment's pause, Teddy's head of golden fur appeared at the top of the stairs.

'Is David in his room, Teddy?'

'David went into the garden, Mummy.'

'Come down here, Teddy!'

She stood impassively, watching the little furry figure as it climbed down from step to step on its stubby limbs. When it reached the bottom, she picked it up and carried it into the living-room. It lay unmoving in her arms, staring up at her. She could feel just the slightest vibration from its motor.

'Stand there, Teddy. I want to talk to you.' She set him down on a tabletop, and he stood as she requested, arms set forward and open in the eternal gesture of embrace.

'Teddy, did David tell you to tell me he had gone into the garden?'

The circuits of the bear's brain were too simple for artifice. 'Yes, Mummy.'

'So you lied to me.'

'Yes, Mummy.'

'*Stop* calling me Mummy! Why is David avoiding me? He's not afraid of me, is he?'

'No. He loves you.'

'Why can't we communicate?'

'David's upstairs.'

The answer stopped her dead. Why waste time talking to this

machine? Why not simply go upstairs and scoop David into her arms and talk to him, as a loving mother should to a loving son? She heard the sheer weight of silence in the house, with a different quality of silence bearing out of every room. On the upper landing, something was moving very silently – David, trying to hide away from her. . . .

He was nearing the end of his speech now. The guests were attentive; so was the Press, lining two walls of the banquetting chamber, recording Henry's words and occasionally photographing him.

'Our serving-man will be, in many senses, a product of the computer. Without computers, we could never have worked through the sophisticated biochemics that go into synthetic flesh. The serving-man will also be an extension of the computer – for he will contain a computer in his own head, a micro-miniaturized computer capable of dealing with almost any situation he may encounter in the home. With reservations, of course.' Laughter at this; many of those present knew the heated debate that had engulfed the Synthank boardroom before the decision had finally been taken to leave the serving-man neuter under his flawless uniform.

'Amid all the triumphs of our civilization – yes, and amid the crushing problems of overpopulation too – it is sad to reflect how many millions of people suffer from increasing loneliness and isolation. Our serving-man will be a boon to them; he will always answer, and the most vapid conversation cannot bore him.

'For the future, we plan more models, male and female – some of them without the limitations of this first one, I promise you! – of more advanced design, true bio-electronic beings.

'Not only will they possess their own computers, capable of individual programming: they will be linked to the World Data Network. Thus everyone will be able to enjoy the equivalent of an Einstein in their own homes. Personal isolation will then be banished for ever!'

He sat down to enthusiastic applause. Even the synthetic serving-man, sitting at the table dressed in an unostentatious suit, applauded with gusto.

Dragging his satchel, David crept round the side of the house. He climbed on to the ornamental seat under the living-room window and peeped cautiously in.

His mother stood in the middle of the room. Her face was blank; its lack of expression scared him. He watched fascinated. He did not move; she did not move. Time might have stopped, as it had stopped in the garden.

At last she turned and left the room. After waiting a moment, David tapped on the window. Teddy looked round, saw him, tumbled off the table, and came over to the window. Fumbling with his paws, he eventually got it open.

They looked at each other.

'I'm no good, Teddy. Let's run away!'

'You're a very good boy. Your Mummy loves you.'

Slowly, he shook his head. 'If she loves me, then why can't I talk to her?'

'You're being silly, David. Mummy's lonely. That's why she has you.'

'She's got Daddy. I've got nobody 'cept you, and I'm lonely.'

Teddy gave him a friendly cuff over the head. 'If you feel so bad, you'd better go to the psychiatrist again.'

'I hate that old psychiatrist – he makes me feel I'm not real.' He started to run across the lawn. The bear toppled out of the window and followed as fast as its stubby legs would allow.

Monica Swinton was up in the nursery. She called to her son once and then stood there, undecided. All was silent.

Crayons lay on his desk. Obeying a sudden impulse, she went over to the desk and opened it. Dozens of pieces of paper lay inside. Many of them were written in crayon in David's clumsy writing, with each letter picked out in a colour different from the letter preceding it. None of the messages was finished.

'MY DEAR MUMMY, HOW ARE YOU REALLY, DO YOU LOVE ME AS MUCH —'

'DEAR MUMMY, I LOVE YOU AND DADDY AND THE SUN IS SHINING —'

'DEAR DEAR MUMMY, TEDDY'S HELPING ME TO WRITE TO YOU. I LOVE YOU AND TEDDY —'

'DARLING MUMMY, I'M YOUR ONE AND ONLY SON AND I LOVE YOU SO MUCH THAT SOME TIMES —'

'DEAR MUMMY, YOU'RE REALLY MY MUMMY AND I HATE

TEDDY —'

'DARLING MUMMY, GUESS HOW MUCH I LOVE —'

'DEAR MUMMY, I'M YOUR LITTLE BOY NOT TEDDY AND I LOVE YOU BUT TEDDY —'

'DEAR MUMMY, THIS IS A LETTER TO YOU JUST TO SAY HOW MUCH HOW EVER SO MUCH —'

Monica dropped the pieces of paper and burst out crying. In their gay inaccurate colours, the letters fanned out and settled on the floor.

Henry Swinton caught the express home in high spirits, and occasionally said a word to the synthetic serving-man he was taking home with him. The serving-man answered politely and punctually, although his answers were not always entirely relevant by human standards.

The Swintons lived in one of the ritziest city-blocks, half a kilometre above the ground. Embedded in other apartments, their apartment had no windows on to the outside; nobody wanted to see the overcrowded external world. Henry unlocked the door with his retina-pattern-scanner and walked in, followed by the serving-man.

At once, Henry was surrounded by the friendly illusion of gardens set in eternal summer. It was amazing what Whologram could do to create huge mirages in small space. Behind its roses and wistaria stood their house: the deception was complete: a Georgian mansion appeared to welcome him.

'How do you like it?' he asked the serving-man.

'Roses occasionally suffer from black spot.'

'These roses are guaranteed free from any imperfections.'

'It is always advisable to purchase goods with guarantees, even if they cost slightly more.'

'Thanks for the information,' Henry said dryly. Synthetic life-forms were less than ten years old, and the old android mechanicals less than sixteen; the faults of their systems were still being ironed out, year by year.

He opened the door and called to Monica.

She came out by the sitting-room immediately and flung her arms round him, kissing him ardently on cheek and lips. Henry was amazed.

Pulling back to look at her face, he saw how she seemed to

generate light and beauty. It was months since he had seen her so excited. Instinctively, he clasped her tighter.

'Darling, what's happened?'

'Henry, Henry – oh, my darling, I was in despair.... But I've dialled the afternoon post and – you'll never believe it! Oh, it's wonderful!'

'For heaven's sake, woman, what's wonderful?'

He caught a glimpse of the heading on the photostat in her hand, still moist from the wall-receiver: Ministry of Population. He felt the colour drain from his face in sudden shock and hope.

'Monica ... oh.... Don't tell me our number's come up!'

'Yes, my darling, yes, we've won this week's parenthood lottery! We can go ahead and conceive a child at once!'

He let out a yell of joy. They danced round the room. Pressure of population was such that reproduction had to be strictly controlled. Childbirth required government permission. For this moment, they had waited four years. Incoherently they cried their delight.

They paused at last, gasping, and stood in the middle of the room to laugh at each other's happiness. When she had come down from the nursery, Monica had de-opaqued the windows, so that they now revealed the vista of garden beyond. Artificial sunlight was growing long and golden across the lawn – and David and Teddy were staring through the window at them.

Seeing their faces, Henry and his wife grew serious.

'What do we do about *them*?' Henry asked.

'Teddy's no trouble. He works well.'

'Is David malfunctioning?'

'His verbal communication-centre is still giving trouble. I think he'll have to go back to the factory again.'

'Okay. We'll see how he does before the baby's born. Which reminds me – I have a surprise for you: help just when help is needed! Come into the hall and see what I've got.'

As the two adults disappeared from the room, boy and bear sat down beneath the standard roses.

'Teddy – I suppose Mummy and Daddy are real, aren't they?'

Teddy said, 'You ask such silly questions, David. Nobody knows what "real" really means. Let's go indoors.'

'First I'm going to have another rose!' Plucking a bright pink flower, he carried it with him into the house. It could lie on the pillow as he went to sleep. Its beauty and softness reminded him of Mummy.

The great diesel train hauled out of Naipur Road, heading grandly south. Jane Pentecouth caught a last glimpse of it over bobbing heads as she followed the stretcher into the station waiting-room.

She pushed her way through the excited crowd, managing to get to her father's side and rejoin the formidable Dr. Chandhari, who had taken charge of the operation.

'My car will come in only a few moments, Miss Pentecouth,' he said, waving away the people who were leaning over the stretcher and curiously touching the sick man. 'It will whisk us to my home immediately, not a mile distant. It was extremely fortunate that I happened to be travelling on the very same express with you.'

'But my father would have been —'

'Do not thank me, dear lady, do not thank me! The pleasure is mine, and your father is saved. I shall do my level best for him.'

She had not been about to thank this beaming and terrifying Hindu. She trembled on the verge of hysterical protest. It was many years since she had felt so helpless. Her father's frightening attack on the train had been bad enough. All those terrible people had flocked round, all offering advice. Then Dr. Chandhari had appeared, taken command, and made the conductor stop the train at Naipur Road, this small station apparently situated in the middle of nowhere, claiming that his home was near by. Irresistibly, Jane had been carried along on the steamy side of solicitude and eloquence.

But she did believe that her father's life had been saved by Dr. Chandhari. Robert Pentecouth was breathing almost normally. She hardly recognized him as she took his hand; he was in a coma. But at least he was still alive, and, in the express, as he bellowed and fought with the coronary attack, she had imagined him about to die.

The crowd surged into the waiting-room, all fighting to lend a hand with the stretcher. It was oppressively hot in the small room; the fan on the ceiling merely caused the heat to circulate.

As more and more men surged into the room, Jane stood up and said loudly, 'Will you all please get out, except for Dr. Chandhari and his secretary!'

The doctor was very pleased by this, seeing that it implied her acceptance of him. He set his secretary to clearing the room, or at least arguing with the crowd that still flocked in. Bending a yet more perfect smile upon her, he said, 'My young intelligent daughter Amma is fortunately at home at this present moment, dear Miss Pentecouth, so you will have some pleasant company just while your father is recovering his health with us.'

She smiled back, thinking to herself that the very next day, when her father had rested, they would return to Calcutta and proper medical care. On that she was determined.

She was impressed by the Chandhari household despite herself.

It was an ugly modernistic building, all cracked concrete outside – bought off a film star who had committed suicide, Amma cheerfully told her. All rooms, including the garage under the house, were air-conditioned. There was a heart-shaped swimming pool at the back, although it was empty of water and the sides were cracked. High white walls guarded the property. From her bedroom, Jane looked over the top of the wall at a dusty road sheltered by palm trees and the picturesque squalor of a dozen hovels, where the small children stood naked in doorways and dogs rooted and snarled in piles of rubbish.

'There is such contrast between rich and poor here,' Jane said, surveying the scene. It was the morning after her arrival here.

'What a very European remark!' said Amma. 'The poor people expect that the doctor should live to a proper standard, or he has no reputation.'

Amma was only twenty, perhaps half Jane's age. An attractive girl, with delicate gestures that made Jane feel clumsy. As she herself explained, she was modern and enlightened, and did not intend to marry until she was older.

'What do you do all day, Amma?' Jane asked.

'I am in the government, of course, but now I am taking a holiday. It is rather boring here, but still I don't mind it for a change. Next week, I will go away from here. What do you do all day, Jane?'

'My father is one of the directors of the new EGNP Trust. I just look after him. He is making a brief tour of India, Pakistan, and Ceylon, to see how the Trust will be administered. I'm afraid the heat and travel have over-taxed him. His breathing has been bad for several days.'

'He is old. They should have sent a younger man.' Seeing the look on Jane's face, she said, 'Please do not take offence! I am meaning only that it is unfair to send a man of his age to our hot climate. What is this trust you are speaking of?'

'The European Gross National Product Trust. Eleven leading European nations contribute 1 per cent of their gross national product to assist development in this part of the world.'

'I see. More help for the poor over-populated Indians, is that so?' The two women looked at each other. Finally, Amma said, 'I will take you out with me this afternoon, and you shall see the sort of people to whom this money of yours will be going, if they live sufficiently long enough.'

'I shall be taking my father back to Calcutta this afternoon.'

'You know my father will not allow that, and he is the doctor. Your father will die if you are foolish enough to move him. You must remain and enjoy our simple hospitality and try not to be too bored.'

'Thank you, I am not bored!' Her life was such that she had had ample training in not being bored. More even than not being in command of the situation, she hated failing to understand the attitude of these people. With what grace she could muster, she told the younger woman, 'If Dr. Chandhari advises that my father should not be moved, then I will be pleased to accompany you this afternoon.'

After the light midday meal, Jane was ready for the outing at two o'clock. But Amma and the car were not ready until almost five o'clock, when the sun was moving towards the west.

Robert Pentecouth lay breathing heavily, large in a small white bed. He was recognizable again, looked younger. Jane did not love him; but she would do anything to preserve his life. That was her considered verdict as she looked down on him. He had gulped down a lot of life in his time.

Something in the room smelt unpleasant. Perhaps it was her

father. By his bedside squatted an old woman in a dull red-and-maroon sari, wrinkled of face, with a jewel like a dried scab screwed in one nostril. She spoke no English. Jane was uneasy with her, not certain whether she was not Chandhari's wife. You heard funny things about Indian wives.

The ceiling was a maze of cracks. It would be the first thing he would see when he opened his eyes. She touched his head and left the room.

Amma drove. A big new car that took the rutted tracks uneasily. There was little to Naipur Road. The ornate and crumbling houses of the main street turned slightly uphill, became mere shacks. The sunlight buzzed. Over the brow of the slope, the village lost heart entirely and died by a huge banyan tree, beneath which an old man sat on a bicycle.

Beyond, cauterized land, a coastal plain lying rumpled, scarred by man's long and weary occupation.

'Only ten miles,' Amma said. 'It gets more pretty later. It's not so far from the ocean, you know. We are going to see an old nurse of mine who is sick.'

'Is there plague in these parts?'

'Orissa has escaped so far. A few cases down in Cuttack. And of course in Calcutta. Calcutta is the home town of the plague. But we are quite safe – my nurse is dying only of a malnutritional disease.'

Jane said nothing.

They had to drive slowly as the track deteriorated. Everything had slowed. People by the tattered roadside stood silently, silently were encompassed by the car's cloud of dust. A battered truck slowly approached, slowly passed. Under the annealing sun, even time had a wound.

Among low hills, little more than undulations of the ground, they crossed a bridge over a dying river and Amma stopped the car in the shade of some deodars. As the women climbed out, a beggar sitting at the base of a tree called out to them for baksheesh, but Amma ignored him. Gesturing courteously to Jane, she said, 'Let us walk under the trees to where the old nurse's family lives. It perhaps would be better if you did not enter the house with me, but I shall not be long. You can look round the village. There is a pleasant temple to see.'

Only a few yards farther on, nodding and smiling, she turned aside and, ducking her head, entered a small house with mud walls.

It was a long blank village, ruled by the sun. Jane felt her isolation as soon as Amma disappeared.

A group of small children with big eyes was following Jane. They whispered to each other but did not approach too closely. A peasant farmer, passing with a thin-ribbed cow, called out to the children. Jane walked slowly, fanning the flies from her face.

She knew this was one of the more favoured regions of India. For all that, the poverty – the stone age poverty – afflicted her. She was glad her father was not with her, in case he felt as she did, that this land could soak up EGNP money as easily, as tracelessly, as it did the monsoon.

Walking under the trees, she saw a band of monkeys sitting or pacing by some more distant huts, and moved nearer to look at them. The huts stood alone, surrounded by attempts at agriculture. A dog nosed by the rubbish heaps, keeping an eye on the monkeys.

Stones were set beneath the big tree where the monkeys paced. Some were painted or stained, and branches of the tree had been painted white. Offerings of flowers lay in a tiny shrine attached to the main trunk; a garland withered on a low branch above a monkey's head. The monkey, Jane saw, suckled a baby at its narrow dugs.

A man stepped from behind the tree and approached Jane.

He made a sign of greeting and said, 'Lady, you want buy somet'ing?'

She looked at him. Something unpleasant was happening to one of his eyes, and flies surrounded it. But he was a well-built man, thin, of course, but not as old as she had at first thought. His head was shaven; he wore only a white dhoti. He appeared to have nothing to sell.

'No, thank you,' she said.

He came closer.

'Lady, you are English lady? You buy small souvenir, some one very nice thing of value for to take with you back to England! Look, I show – you are please to wait here one minute.'

He turned and ducked into the most dilapidated of the huts.

She looked about, wondering whether to stay. In a moment, the man emerged again into the sun, carrying a vase. The children gathered and stared silently; only the monkeys were restless.

'This is very lovely Indian vase, lady, bought in Jamshedpur, very fine hand manufacture. Perceive beautiful artistry work, lady!'

She hesitated before taking the poor brass vase in her hands. He turned and called sharply into the hut, and then redoubled his sales talk. He had been a worker in a shoe factory in Jamshedpur, he told her, but the factory had burned down and he could find no other work. He had brought his wife and children here, to live with his brother.

'I'm afraid I'm not interested in buying the vase,' she said.

'Lady, please, you give only ten rupees! Ten rupees only!' He broke off.

His wife had emerged from the hut, to stand without motion by his side. In her arms, she carried a child.

The child looked solemnly at Jane from its giant dark eyes. It was naked except for a piece of rag, over which a great belly sagged. Its body, and especially the face and skull, were covered in pustules, from some of which a liquid seeped. Its head had been smeared with ash. The baby did not move or cry; what its age was, Jane could not estimate.

Its father had fallen silent for a moment. Now he said, 'My child is having to die, lady, look see! You give me ten rupees.'

Now she shrank from the proffered vase. Inside the hut, there were other children stirring in the shadows. The sick child looked outwards with an expression of great wisdom and beauty – or so Jane interpreted it – as if it understood and forgave all things. Its very silence frightened her, and the stillness of the mother. She backed away, feeling chilled.

'No, no, I don't want the vase! I must go —'

Muttering her excuses, she turned away and hurried, almost ran, back towards the car. She could hear the man calling to her.

She climbed into the car. The man came and stood outside, not touching the car, apologetic, explaining, offering the vase for only eight rupees, talking, talking. Seven-and-a-half rupees. Jane hid her face.

When Amma emerged, the man backed away, said something

meekly; Amma replied sharply. He turned, clutching the vase, and the children watched. She climbed into the driving seat and started the car.

'He tried to sell me something. A vase. It was the only thing he had to sell, I suppose,' Jane said. 'He wasn't rude.' She felt the silent gears of their relationship change; she could no longer pretend to superiority, since she had been virtually rescued. After a moment, she asked. 'What was the matter with his child? Did he tell you?'

'He is a man of the scheduled classes. His child is dying of the smallpox. There is always smallpox in the villages.'

'I imagined it was the plague. . . .'

'I told you, we do not have the plague in Orissa yet.'

The drive home was a silent one, voiceless in the corroded land. The people moving slowly home had long shadows now. When they arrived at the gates of the Chandhari house, a porter was ready to open the gate, and a distracted servant stood there; she ran fluttering beside the car, calling to Amma.

Amma turned and said, 'Jane, I am sorry to tell you that your father has had another heart attack just now.'

The attack was already over. Robert Pentecouth lay unconscious on the bed, breathing raspingly. Doctor Chandhari stood looking down at him and sipping an iced lime-juice. He nodded tenderly at Jane as she moved to the bedside.

'I have of course administered an anti-coagulant, but your father is very ill, Miss Pentecouth,' he said. 'There is severe cardiac infarction, together with weakness in the mitral valve, which is situated at the entrance of the left ventricle. This has caused congestion of the lungs, which means the trouble of breathlessness, very much accentuated by the hot atmosphere of the Indian sub-continent. I have done my level best for him.'

'I must get him home, doctor.'

Chandhari shook his head. 'The air journey will be severely taxing on him. I tell you frankly I do not imagine for a single moment that he will survive it.'

'What should I do, doctor? I'm so frightened!'

'Your father's heart is badly scarred and damaged, dear lady. He needs a new heart, or he will give up the ghost.'

Jane sat down on the chair by the bedside and said, 'We are

in your hands.'

He was delighted to hear it. 'There are no safer hands, dear Miss Pentecouth.' He gazed at them with some awe as he said, 'Let me outline a little plan of campaign for you. Tomorrow we put your father on the express to Calcutta. I can phone to Naipur Road station to have it stop. Do not be alarmed! I will accompany you on the express. At the Radakhrishna General Hospital in Howrah in Calcutta is that excellent man, K. V. Menon, who comes from Trivandrum, as does my own family – a very civilized and clever man of the Nair caste. K. V. Menon. His name is widely renowned and he will perform the operation.'

'Operation, doctor?'

'Certainly, certainly! He will give a new heart. K. V. Menon has performed many many successful heart-transplants. The operation is as commonplace in Calcutta as in California. Do not worry! And I will personally stand by you all the while. Perhaps Amma shall come too because I see you are firm friends already. Good, good, don't worry!'

In his excitement, he took her by the arm and made her rise to her feet. She stood there, solid but undecided, staring at him.

'Come!' he said. 'Let us go and telephone all the arrangements! We will make some commotion around these parts, eh? Your father is okay here with the old nurse-woman to watch. In a few days, he will wake up with a new heart and be well again.'

Jane sent a cable explaining the situation to the Indian headquarters of EGNP in Delhi (the city which ancient colonialist promptings had perhaps encouraged the authorities to choose). Then she stood back while the commotion spread.

It spread first to the household. More people were living in the Chandhari house than Jane had imagined. She met the doctor's wife, an elegant sari-clad woman who spoke good English and who apparently lived in her own set of rooms, together with her servants. The latter came and went, enlivened by the excitement. Messengers were despatched to the bazaar for various little extra requirements.

The commotion rapidly spread farther afield. People came to

inquire the health of the white sahib, to learn the worst for themselves. The representative of the local newspaper called. Another doctor arrived, and was taken by Dr. Chandhari, a little proudly, to inspect the patient.

If anything, the commotion grew after darkness fell.

Jane went to sit by her father. He was still unconscious. Once, he spoke coherently, evidently imagining himself back in England; although she answered him, he gave no sign that he heard. Amma came in to say good-night on her way to bed.

'We shall be leaving early in the morning,' Jane said. 'My father and I have brought you only trouble. Please don't come to Calcutta with us. It isn't necessary.'

'Of course not. I will come only to Naipur Road station. I'm glad if we could help at all. And with a new heart, your father will be really hale and hearty again. Menon is a great expert in heart-transplantation.'

'Yes. I have heard his name, I think. You never told me, Amma – how did you find your old nurse this afternoon?'

'You did not ask me. Unhappily, she died during last night.'

'Oh! I'm so sorry!'

'Yes, it is hard for her family. Already they are much in debt to the moneylender.'

She left the room; shortly after, Jane also retired. But she could not sleep. After an hour or two of fitful sleep, she got dressed again and went downstairs, obsessed with a mental picture of the glass of fresh lime-juice she had seen the doctor drinking. She could hear unseen people moving about in rooms she had never entered. In the garden, too, flickering tongues of light moved. A heart-transplant was still a strange event in Naipur Road, as it had once been in Europe and America; perhaps it would have even more superstition attached to it here than it had there.

When a servant appeared, she made her request. After long delay, he brought the glass on a tray, gripping it so that it would not slip, and lured her out on to the veranda with it. She sat in a wicker chair and sipped it. A face appeared in the garden, a hand reached in supplication up to her.

'Please! Miss Lady!'

Startled, she recognized the man with the dying child to whom she had spoken the previous afternoon.

The next morning, Jane was roused by one of the doctor's servants. Dazed after too little sleep, she dressed and went down to drink tea. She could find nothing to say; her brain had not woken yet. Amma and her father talked continuously in English to each other.

The big family car was waiting outside. Pentecouth was gently loaded in, and the luggage piled round him. It was still little more than dawn; as Jane, Amma, and Chandhari climbed in and the car rolled forward, wraithlike figures were moving already. A cheerful little fire burned here and there inside a house. A tractor rumbled towards the fields. People stood at the sides of the road, numb, to let the car pass. The air was chilly; but, in the eastern sky, the banners of the day's warmth were already violently flying.

They were almost at the railway station when Jane turned to Amma. 'That man with the child dying of smallpox walked all the way to the house to speak to me. He said he came as soon as he heard of my father's illness.'

'The servants had no business to let him through the gate. That is how diseases spread,' Amma said.

'He had something else to sell me last night. Not a vase. He wanted to sell his heart!'

Amma laughed. 'The vase would be a better bargain, Jane!'

'How can you laugh? He was so desperate to help his wife and family. He wanted fifty rupees. He would take the money back to his wife and then he would come with us to the Calcutta Hospital to have his heart cut out!'

Putting her hand politely to her mouth, Amma laughed again.

'Why is it funny?' Jane asked desperately. 'He meant what he said. Everything was so black for him that his life was worth only fifty rupees!'

'But his life is not worth so much, by far!' Amma said. 'He is just a village swindler. And the money would not cure the child, in any case. The type of smallpox going about here is generally fatal, isn't it, Pappa?'

Dr. Chandhari, who sat with a hand on his patient's forehead, said, 'This man's idea is of course not scientific. He is one of the scheduled classes – an Untouchable, as we used to say. He has never eaten very much all during his life and so he will have only a little weak heart. It would never be a good heart in your father's body, to circulate all his blood properly.' With a proud gesture, he thumped Robert Pentecouth's chest. 'This is the body of the well-nourished man. In Calcutta, we shall find him a proper big heart that will do the work effectively.'

They arrived at the railway station. The sun was above the horizon and climbing rapidly. Rays of gold poured through the branches of the trees by the station on to the faces of people arriving to watch the great event, the stopping of the great Madras–Calcutta express, and the loading aboard of a white man going for a heart-transplant.

Furtively, Jane looked about the crowd, searching to see if her man happened to be there. But, of course, he would be back in his village by now, with his wife and the children.

Intercepting the look, Amma said, 'Jane, you did not give that man baksheesh, did you?'

Jane dropped her gaze, not wishing to betray herself.

'He would have robbed you,' Amma insisted. 'His heart would be valueless. These people are never free from hook-worms, you know – in the heart and the stomach. You should have bought the vase if you wanted a souvenir of Naipur Road – not a heart, for goodness sake!'

The train was coming. The crowd stirred. Jane took Amma's hand. 'Say no more. I will always have memories of Naipur Road.'

She busied herself about her father's stretcher as the great sleek train growled into the station.

Being alone in the house, not feeling too well, I kept the television burning for company. The volume was low. Three men mouthed almost soundlessly about the Chinese rôle in the Vietnam war. Getting my head down, I turned to my aunt Laura's manuscript.

She had a new hairstyle these days. She looked very good; she was seventy-three, my aunt, and you were not intended to take her for anything less; but you could mistake her for ageless. Now she had written her first book – 'a sort of autobiography', she told me when she handed the bundle over. Terrible apprehension gripped me. I had to rest my head in my hand. Another heart attack coming.

On the screen, figures scrambling over mountain. All unclear. Either my eyesight going or a captured Chinese newsreel. Strings of animals – you couldn't see what, film slightly overexposed. Could be reindeer crossing snow, donkeys crossing sand. I could hear them now, knocking, knocking, very cold.

A helicopter crashing towards the ground? Manuscript coming very close, my legs, my lips, the noise I was making.

There was a ship embedded in the ice. You'd hardly know there was a river. Snow had piled up over the piled-up ice. Surrounding land was flat. There was music, distorted stuff from a radio, accordions, and balalaikas. The music came from a wooden house. From its misty windows, they saw the ship, sunk in the rotted light. A thing moved along the road, clearing away the day's load of ice, ugly in form and movement. Four people sat in the room with the unpleasant music; two of them were girls in their late teens, flat faces with sharp eyes; they were studying at the university. Their parents ate a salad, two forks, one plate. Both man and woman had been imprisoned in a nearby concentration camp in Stalin's time. The camp had gone now. Built elsewhere, for other reasons.

The ship was free of ice, sailing along in a sea of mist. It was no longer a pleasure ship but a research ship. Men were singing.

They sang that they sailed on a lake as big as Australia.

'They aren't men. They are horses!' My aunt.

'There are horses aboard.'

'I certainly don't see any men.'

'Funny-looking horses.'

'Did you see a wolf then?'

'I mean, more like ponies. Shaggy. Small and shaggy. Is that gun loaded?'

'Naturally. They're forest ponies – I mean to say, not ponies but reindeer. "The curse of the devil", they call them.'

'It's the bloody rotten light! They do look like reindeer. But they must be men.'

'Ever looked one in the eye? They are *the* most frightening animals.'

My father was talking to me again, speaking over the phone. It had been so long. I had forgotten how I loved him, how I missed him. All I remembered was that I had gone with my two brothers to his funeral; but that must have been someone else's funeral, someone else's father. So many people, good people, were dying.

I poured my smiles down the telephone, heart full of delight, easy. He was embarking on one of his marvellous stories. I gulped down his sentences.

'That burial business was all a joke – a swindle. I collected two thousand pounds for that, you know, Bruce. No, I'm lying! Two and a half. It was chicken feed, of course, compared with some of the swindles I've been in. Did I ever tell you how Ginger Robbins and I got demobbed in Singapore at the end of the war, 1945? We bought a defunct trawler off a couple of Chinese business men – very nice old fatties called Pee – marvellous name! Ginger and I had both kept our uniforms, and we marched into a transit camp and got a detail of men organized – young rookies, all saluting us like mad – you'd have laughed! We got them to load a big LCT engine into a five-tonner, and we all drove out of camp without a question being asked, and – wham! – straight down to the docks and our old tub. It was boiling bloody hot, and you should have seen those squaddies sweat as they unloaded the engine and man-handled —'

'Shit, Dad, this is all very funny and all that,' I said, 'but I've got some work to do, you know. Don't think I'm not enjoying a great reminiscence, but I have to damned work, see? Okay?'

I rang off.

I put my head between my hands and – no, I could not manage weeping. I just put my head between my hands and wondered why I did what I did. Subconscious working, of course. I tried to plan out a science fiction story about a race of men who had only subconsciouses. Their consciousnesses had been painlessly removed by surgery.

They moved faster without their burdening consciousnesses, wearing lunatic smiles or lunatic frowns. Directly after the operation, scars still moist, they had restarted World War II, some assuming the rôles of Nazis or Japanese or Jugoslav partisans or British fighter pilots in kinky boots. Many even chose to be Italians, the rôle of Mussolini being so keenly desired that at one time there were a dozen Duces striding about, keeping company with the droves of Hitlers.

Some of these Hitlers later volunteered to fly with the Kamakazis.

Many women volunteered to be raped by the Wehrmacht and turned nasty when the requirements were filled. When a concentration camp was set up, it was rapidly filled; people have a talent for suffering. The history of the war was rewritten a bit. They had Passchendale and the Somme in; a certain President Johnson led the British forces.

The war petered out in a win for Germany. Few people were left alive. They voted themselves second-class citizens, mostly becoming Jewish Negroes or Vietnamese. There was birching between consenting adults. These good folk voted unanimously to have their subconsciousnesses removed, leaving only their ids.

I was on the floor. My study. The name of the vinolay was – it had a name, that rather odious pattern of little wooden chocks. I had it on the tip of my tongue. When I sat up, I realized how cold I was, cold and trembling, not working very well.

My body was rather destructive to society, as the Top Clergy would say. I had used it for all sorts of things; nobody knew where it had been. I had used it in an unjust war. Festival. It was called Festival. Terrible name, surely impeded sales.

I could not get up. I crawled across the floor towards the drink cupboard in the next room. Vision blurry. As I looked up, I saw my old aunt's manuscript on the table. One sheet had fluttered down on to the Festival. I crawled out into the dining-room, through the door, banging myself as I went. Neither mind nor body was the precision ballistic missile it once had been.

The bottle. I got it open before I saw it was Sweet Martini, and dropped it. It seeped into the carpet; no doubt that had a name too. Weary, I rested my head in the mess.

'If I die now, I shall never read Aunt Laura's life. . . .'

Head on carpet, bottom in air, I reached and grasped the whisky bottle. Why did they make the stuff so hard to get at? Then I drank. It made me very ill indeed.

It was Siberia again, the dread reindeer sailing eternally their ships across the foggy ice lakes. They were munching things, fur and wood and bone, the saliva freezing into icicles as it ran from their jaws. Terrible noise, like the knocking of my heart.

I was laughing. Whoever died dreaming of reindeer – who but Lapps? Digging my fingers into the nameless carpet, I tried to sit up. It proved easier to open my eyes.

In the shady room, a woman was sitting. She had turned from the window to look at me. Gentle and reassuring lines and planes composed her face. It took a while to see it as a face; even as an arrangement against a window, I greatly liked it.

The woman came over to look closely at me. I realized I was in bed before I realized it was my wife. She touched my brow, making my nervous system set to work on discovering whether the signal was a pain or pleasure impulse, so that things in there were too busy for me to hear what she was saying. The sight of her speaking was pleasurable; it moved me to think that I should answer her.

'How's Aunt Laura?'

The messages were coming through, old old learning sorting out speech, hearing, vision, tactile sensations, and shunting them through the appropriate organs. The doctor had been; it had only been a slight one, but this time I really would have to rest up and take all the pills and do nothing foolish; she had already phoned the office and they were very understanding.

One of my brothers was coming round, but she was not at all
sure whether he should be allowed to see me. I felt entirely as
she did about that.

'I've forgotten what it was called.'

'Your brother Bob?'

My speech was a little indistinct. I had a creepy feeling about
whether I could move the limbs I knew were bundled with me
in the bed. We'd tackle that challenge as and when necessary.

'Not Bob. Not Bob. The . . . the. . . .'

'Just lie there quietly, darling. Don't try to talk.'

'The . . . carpet. . . .'

She went on talking. The hand on the forehead was a good
idea. Irritably, I wondered why she didn't do it to me when I
was well and better able to appreciate it. What the hell was it
called? Roundabout?

'Roundabout. . . .'

'Yes, darling. You've been here for several hours, you know.
You aren't quite awake yet, are you?'

'Shampoo. . . .'

'Later, perhaps. Lie back now and have another little doze.'

'Variety. . . .'

'Try and have another little doze.'

One of the difficulties of being a publisher is that one has to
fend off so many manuscripts submitted by friends of friends.
Friends alway have friends with obsessions about writing. Life
would be simple – it was the secret of a happy life, not to have
friends of friends. Supposing you were cast away on a desert
island disc, Mr. Hartwell, what eight friends of friends would
you take with you, provided you had an inexhaustible supply of
manuscripts?

I leaned across the desk and said, 'But this is worse than ever.
You aren't even a friend of a friend of a friend, auntie.'

'And what am I if I'm *not* a friend of a friend?'

'Well, you're an aunt of a nephew, you see, and after all, as an
old-established firm, we have to adhere to certain rules of –
etiquette, shall we call it, by which —'

It was difficult to see how offended she was. The pile of
manuscript hid most of her face from view. I could not remove
it, partly because there was a certain awareness that this was

really the sheets. Finally I got them open.

'It's your life, Bruce. I've written your life. It could be a best-seller.'

'Variety.... No, Show Business....'

'I thought of calling it "By Any Other Name"....'

'We have to adhere to certain rules....'

It was better when I woke again. I had the name I had been searching for: Festival. Now I could not remember what it was the name of.

The bedroom had changed. There were flowers about. The portable TV set stood on the dressing-table. The curtains were drawn back and I could see into the garden. My wife was still there, coming over, smiling. Several times she walked across to me, smiling. The light came and went, the flowers changed position, colour, the doctor got in her way. Finally she reached me.

'You've made it! You're marvellous!'

'*You've* made it! *You're* marvellous!'

No more trouble after that. We had the TV on and watched the war escalate in Vietnam and Cambodia.

Returning health made me philosophical. 'That's what made me ill. Nothing I did ... under-exercise, over-eating ... too much booze ... too many fags ... just the refugees.'

'I'll turn it off if it upsets you.'

'No. I'm adapting. They won't get me again. It's the misery the TV sets beam out from Vietnam all over the world. That's what gives people heart attacks. Look at lung cancer – think how it has been on the increase since the war started out there. They aren't real illnesses in the old sense, they're sort of prodromic illness, forecasting some bigger sickness to come. The whole world's going to escalate into a Vietnam.'

She jumped up, alarmed. 'I'll switch it off!'

'The war?'

'The set.'

The screen went blank. I could still see them. Thin women in those dark blue overalls, all their possessions slung from a frail bamboo over a frail shoulder. Father had died about the time the French were slung out. We were all bastards. Perhaps every time one of us died, one of the thin women lived. I began to dream up a new religion.

They had the angels dressed in UN uniform. They no longer looked like angels, not because of the uniform but because they were all disguised as a western diplomat – nobody in particular, but jocular, uneasy, stolid, with stoney eyes that twinkled.

My angel came in hotfoot and said, 'Can you get a few friends of friends together? The refugees are waiting on the beach.'

There were four of us in the hospital beds. We scrambled up immediately, dragging bandages and sputum cups and bed pans. The guy next to me came trailing a plasma bottle. We climbed into the helicopter.

We prayed en route. 'Bet the Chinese and Russian volunteers don't pray on the trip.' I insinuated to the angel.

'The Chinese and Russians don't volunteer.'

'So you make a silly insinuation, you get a silly innuendo,' the plasma man said.

God's hand powered the chopper. Faster than engines but maybe less reliable. We landed on the beach beside a foaming river. Heat pouring down and up the sideways. The refugees were forlorn and dirty. A small boy stood hatless with a babe hatless on his back. Both ageless, eyes like reindeer's, dark, moist, cursed.

'I'll die for those two,' I said, pointing.

'One for one. Which one do you choose?'

'Hell, come on now, angel, isn't my soul as good as any two god-damned Viet kid souls?'

'No discounts here, bud. Yours is shop-soiled, anyway.'

'Okay, the bigger kid.'

He was whisked instantly into the helicopter. I saw his dirty and forlorn face at the window. The baby sprawled screaming on the sand. It was naked, scabs on both knees. It yelled in slow motion, piddling, trying to burrow into the sand. I reached slowly out to it, but the exchange had been made, the angel turned the napalm on to me. As I fell, the baby went black in my shadow.

'Let me switch the fire down, if you're too hot, darling.'

'Yuh. And a drink. . . .'

She helped me struggle into a sitting position, put her arm round my shoulders. Glass to lips, teeth, cool water in throat.

'Go, I love you, Ellen, thank God you're not. . . .'

'What? Another nightmare?'

'Not Vietnamese. . . .'

It was better then, and she sat and talked about what had been going on, who had called, my brother, my secretary, the Roaches . . . 'the Roaches have called' . . . 'any Earwigs'? . . . the neighbours, the doctor. Then we were quiet a while.

'I'm better now, much better. The older generation's safe from all this, honey. They were born as civilians. We weren't. Get me auntie's manuscript, will you?'

'You're not starting work this week.'

'It won't hurt me. She'll be writing about her past, before the war and all that. The past's safe. It'll do me good. The prose style doesn't matter.'

I settled back as she left the room. Flowers stood before the TV, making it like a little shrine.

I'd visited the exhibition of paintings by William Holman Hunt at the Victoria & Albert Museum. Afterwards, I went to the cafeteria, sitting and drinking orangeade after orangeade. A woman of about fifty sat down opposite me, we exchanged a word about the beautiful summer weather, and she embarked immediately upon the story of her life, which had been full of trouble and three husbands; not to mention a spaniel that got run over on the Kingston Bypass.

In Hunt's work, we are meant to think of the surface of the canvas as non-existent – a conspiracy that no longer exists between modern painters and their audience. Each frame admits one to a little floodlit stage. Inside lies a diorama in bright colour. In a picture like *The Apple Harvest,* you look at the apples, rosily hanging between the girl's basket and the sack, and peer closer for the threads that keep them suspended so miraculously in mid-air. With Hunt, you never see the threads.

Her first husband was pretty rich. He was a tea-planter, with plantations out in Assam. She told me how many workers they employed. Even in the hills, the climate was too hot for her. Perhaps it was the hot London day that prompted her reminiscences. Anyhow, he died out in Assam, and so she'd had to come home alone. But on the boat back from Bombay, she had met Albert. She lit a cigarette and companionably blew the smoke at me.

My interest in Holman Hunt extends over many years. In some ways, he must have been like me – for instance, all that nonsense about actually transporting a goat to the shores of the Dead Sea to paint it! That is the sort of thing I might get involved in myself. But as a writer I also respond to what I diagnose as his dilemma. That novel of mine, *Report on Probability A,* the one that didn't cause such a fuss, centred round Hunt's best painting, *The Hireling Shepherd.*

I have been to Bombay too, but I didn't tell her that. By now, she needed no prompting. This chap Albert was apparently an authority on butterflies. Would anyone ever refer to me as 'an authority on Holman Hunt'? I tried to visualize my first wife chumming up with some fellow in a cafeteria, rattling off her tribulations, among which I imagine I would figure prominently, and saying, 'He was quite an authority on Holman Hunt'. No, that would be allowing me too much.

My intention was to write a review of the exhibition. Perhaps this is where the only parallel between Hunt and me comes in, and that is a fairly tenuous one. Hunt was right at the fag-end of one tradition, the Renaissance tradition of lining up acceptable objects in an ideal arrangement and painting them, allowing the spectator an essential rôle in completing the arrangement. And all the while, photography was creeping up on him; men like Degas and Toulouse-Lautrec were making what went on inside the frame its own reference; later still, the Cubists would explore the actual surface of the canvas.

On the other hand, Hunt was quietly revolutionary in his handling of backgrounds. ('I paint,' he said, 'direct on the canvas itself, with every detail I can see, and with the sunlight brightness of the day itself'.) Some of his setting could come from Salvador Dali, and seem almost mescalin-influenced. The tremendous country round the Dead Sea is a case in point; Hunt embraced its surrealist qualities.

'Can I get you an orangeade? I'm going to have another myself.'

'I shouldn't really. I ought to be going. I'm supposed to be meeting my sister at Harrods.'

I bought it for her anyway. I hoped that while I was at the counter she would notice the book I was carrying about with me – Nigel Calder's *Technopolis* – but she was too involved in her own affairs to dwell on all my marvellous paradoxes. I should have said to her, 'Look, isn't it typical of the versatility of people today that I should be so fascinated in the uses or abuses of science, and so obsessed with the present unrolling into the future, and yet remain preoccupied with – well, frankly, not first-rate painters like Holman Hunt!' At times it is hard to see where such conflicting interests integrate. Hunt had the same sort of battle between religion (he was very High Church) and paintings. Perhaps the painting lost. Born a generation later, he might have been more successful.

Hunt was so misunderstood that he took to printing little pamphlets to accompany each painting, explaining what he was doing. He tried to make everything simple. In that respect creators and critics are alike: all strive to make things either simpler or more complex. I only wish some of our critics could be humbler; one wants criticism and not autobiography, but surely it would be realistic if a critic occasionally said, 'My entirely derogatory judgements on Holman Hunt must not be considered in any way definitive, as I was distracted just after the viewing by a woman whose third husband is still alive but separated from her and now living, as far as is known, in a village eight miles from the centre of Torquay.'

As for *Technopolis*, I have been distracted in reviewing that. Calder is writing about ways in which society can control technology. He admits that a scientific policy is difficult to formulate, because the politicians can never look as far ahead in these matters as they need to do. Presumably this explains why nothing coherent is done about the population explosion, like phasing out family allowances, for example. But my mind keeps wandering off the subject; I have to confess I am curious about how the doctors cured her daughter Irene's harelip. She gives me plenty of detail but not the sort of detail I want. Like Hunt, in a way.

We are going to find it difficult to control the course of science and technology, which by now have got a bit set in their ways. We are still faced with problems that were already confronting the Victorians. When Hunt exhibited *The Hireling Shepherd* in the Royal Academy in 1852, the familiar ambivalent attitude to the machine was already established. Since there is no danger that any of my present readers have heard of *Report on Probability A*, I might as well say that one of my themes was a paralysis of time, which I pretended to detect and find exemplified in the anecdotalism of this canvas, and similar Victorian paintings. This poor woman sitting opposite me – she's not going to touch that orangeade I brought her – represents a personal paralysis of time. She's reliving her earlier days over and over. This whole package-deal of her life is no doubt trotted out to strangers every day. Her life may have become the fearful mess it is simply because she thinks backwards instead of forwards. Hunt kept thinking back to the Early Church instead of forward to the Impressionists. Isn't his sun breaking through the cypress trees in the Fiesole canvas of 1868 as fresh in its way as Monet's studies of light and shadow on the Seine, painted in the same year? I suppose the answer is, No, it is not. Just as this woman's remembrance of things past is not a patch on Proust's, though she may have suffered as much.

Here we sit, then: Hunt and she and Calder and me. Calder's in the best position; his time escape-route lies in the future, because his book is not even published till next week; nor does he exactly address himself to the denizens of the V & A canteen. But the rest of us are paralysed by time. So's her sister, stuck in Harrods waiting for her. And her third husband, down outside Torquay. As for me ... has any critic before ever tried to arrive at an objective viewpoint in similar circumstances *and admitted it*? Critics ought to confide more, the way this woman does; we need to know more often what's in it for them.

What's in it for her? She didn't even go to look at the Hunts. She says she doesn't like paintings much. She did when she was a little girl. What the hell's she doing here anyway? I shouldn't have imagined she came to the V & A especially to revel in the delights of the cafeteria. Not with orangeade at one-and-three a carton. Perhaps she comes every morning – captive audience always on tap. I must break away. I notice she tells me everybody's name but her own. This hysterectomy she's telling me about now – would she be so liberal with the gruesome detail if we had been properly introduced? No painter has ever painted a hysterectomy, to my knowledge.

Some awful academic social realistic painter in Moscow – he must have done it. Glaring light; thick-set surgeons; anaesthetists in green overalls; devoted proletarian nurses, almost sexless; scalpels gleaming, the op nearly over; bust of Lenin in the background, surrounded by flags; the womb emerging; general moral uplift. Or perhaps the Russians consider it a decadent capitalist operation. The way she tells it, they're right!

Anyway, Hunt, William Holman. My review. Primarily a religious painter. More competent than his colleague Millais. The only one of the Pre-Raphaelite Brethren to stick to his principles. I came away from his canvases primed with the suspicion – no, confirmed in my opinion that, while he may be by no means the greatest of the Victorian painters, Hunt's place is assured – no, it is the colourist rather than the moralist that today – no, no, no. ... This woman's making more sense than I am. I came away still feeling a strong bond with Hunt. One of the great comic painters: comic-macabre, as *The Shadow of Death* proves. Born too late. Too early. Nothing but cliché ... I must escape from this cliché of a life unrolling before me ... Majorca to recover, indeed! There she met this rich Spaniard. If only one could suspect her of lying. That uncomfortable pause between life and art is not for her, any more than it was for Hunt.

She's on about sex all the time, you notice, without actually daring to tackle the subject head-on. Dear God, we all live out such muddled lives, and so many lives at once. Calder should write a book about controlling *us*!

Hurriedly, I swig down her untouched orangeade and make off with scarcely a farewell, heading towards Harrods, where my wife awaits me.

The inhabitants of the planet Myrin have much to endure from Earthmen, inevitably perhaps, since they represent the only intelligent life we have so far found in the galaxy. The Tenth Research Fleet has already left for Myrin. Meanwhile, some of the fruits of earlier expeditions are ripening.

As has already been established, the superior Myrinian culture, the so-called Confluence of Headwaters, is somewhere in the region of eleven million (Earth) years old, and its language, Confluence, had been established even longer. The etymological team of the Seventh Research Fleet was privileged to sit at the feet of two gentlemen of the Oeldrid Stance Academy. They found that Confluence is a language-cum-posture, and that meanings of words can be radically modified or altered entirely by the stance assumed by the speaker. There is, therefore, no possibility of ever compiling a one-to-one dictionary of English-Confluence, Confluence-English words.

Nevertheless, the list of Confluent words that follows disregards the stances involved, which number almost nine thousand and are all named, and merely offers a few definitions, some of which must be regarded as tentative. The definitions are, at this early stage of our knowledge of the Myrinian culture, valuable in themselves, not only because they reveal something of the inadequacy of our own language, but because they throw some light on to the mysteries of an alien culture. The romanized phonetic system employed is that suggested by Dr. Rohan Harbottle, one of the members of the etymological team of the Seventh Research Fleet, without whose generous assistance this short list could never have been compiled.

AB WE TEL MIN: The sensation that one neither agrees nor disagrees with what is being said to one, but that one simply wishes to depart from the presence of the speaker

ARN TUTKHAN: Having to rise early before anyone else is about; addressing a machine

BAGI RACK: Apologizing as a form of attack; a stick resembling a gun

BAG RACK: Needless and offensive apologies

BAMAN: The span of a man's consciousness

BI: The name of the mythical northern cockerel; a reverie that lasts for more than twenty (Earth) years

BI SAN: A reverie lasting more than twenty years and of a religious nature

BI SAN: A reverie lasting more than twenty years and of a blasphemous nature

BI TOSI: A reverie lasting more than twenty years on cosmological themes

BI TVAS: A reverie lasting more than twenty years on geological themes

BIUI TOSI: A reverie lasting more than a hundred and forty-two years on cosmological themes; the sound of air in a cavern; long dark hair

BIUT TASH: A reverie lasting more than twenty years on Har Dar Ka themes

CANO LEE MIN: Things sensed out-of-sight that will return

CA PATA VATUZ: The taste of a maternal grandfather

CHAM ON TH ZAM: Being witty when nobody else appreciates it

DAR AYRHOH: The garments of an ancient crone; the age-old supposition that Myrin is a hypothetical place

EN IO PLAY: The deliberate dissolving of the senses into sleep

GEE KUTCH: Solar empathy

GE NU: The sorrow that overtakes a mother knowing her child will be born dead

GE NUP DIMU: The sorrow that overtakes the child in the womb when it knows it will be born dead

GOR A: Ability to live for eight hundred years

HA ATUZ SHAK EAN: Disgrace attending natural death of maternal grandfather

HAR DAR KA: The complete understanding that all the soil of Myrin passes through the bodies of its earth-worms every ten years

HAR DI DI KAL: A small worm; the hypothetical creator of a hypothetical sister planet of Myrin

HE YUP: The first words the computers spoke, meaning, 'The light will not be necessary'

HOLT CHA: The feeling of delight that precedes and precipitates wakening

HOLT CHE : The autonomous marshalling of the senses which produces the feeling of delight that precedes and precipitates wakening

HOZ STAP SAN : A writer's attitude to fellow writers

JILY JIP TUP : A thinking machine that develops a stammer; the action of pulling on the trousers while running uphill

JIL JIPY TUP : Any machine with something incurable about it; pleasant laughter that is nevertheless unwelcome; the action of pulling up the trousers while running downhill

KARNAD EES : The enjoyment of a day or a year by doing nothing; fasting

KARNDAL CHESS : The waste of a day or a year by doing nothing; fasting

KARNDOLI YON TOR : Mystical state attained through inaction; feasting; a learned paper on the poetry of metal

KARNDOL KI REE : The waste of a life by doing nothing; a type of fasting

KUNDULUM : To be well and in bed with two pretty sisters

LAHAH SHIP : Tasting fresh air after one has worked several hours at one's desk

LA YUN UN : A struggle in which not a word is spoken; the underside of an inaccessible boulder; the part of one's life unavailable to other people

LEE KE MIN : Anything or anyone out-of-sight that one senses will never return; an apology offered for illness

LIKL INK TH KUTI : The small engine that attends to one after the act of excretion

MAL : A feeling of being watched from within

MAN NAIZ TH : Being aware of electricity in wires concealed in the walls

MUR ON TIG WON : The disagreeable experience of listening to oneself in the middle of a long speech and neither understanding what one is saying nor enjoying the manner in which it is being said; a foreign accent; a lion breaking wind after the evening repast

NAM ON A : The remembrance, in bed, of camp fires

NO LEE LE MUN : The love of a wife that becomes especially vivid when she is almost out-of-sight

NU CROW : Dying before strangers

NU DI DIMU : Dying in a low place, often of a low fever

NU HIN DER VLAK : The invisible stars; forms of death

NUN MUM : Dying before either of one's parents; ceasing to fight just because one's enemy is winning

NUT LAP ME : Dying of laughing

NUT LA POM : Dying laughing

NUT VATO : Managing to die standing up; statues; thorns

NUTVU BAG RACK : To be born dead

NU VALK : Dying deliberately in a lonely (high) place

OBI DAKT : An obstruction; three or more machines talking together

ORAN MUDA : A change of government; an old peasant saying meaning, 'The dirt in the river is different every day'

PAN WOL LE MUDA : A certainty that tomorrow will much resemble today; a line of manufacturing machines

PAT O BANE BAN : The ten heartbeats preceding the first heartbeat of orgasm

PI KI SKAB WE : The parasite that afflicts man and Tig Gag in its various larval stages and, while burrowing in the brain of the Tig Gag, causes it to speak like a man

PI SHAK RACK CHANO : The retrogressive dreams of autumn attributed to the presence in the bloodstream of Pi Ki Skab We

PIT HOR : Pig's cheeks, or the droppings of pigs; the act of name-dropping

PLAY : The heightening of consciousness that arises when one awakens in a strange room that one cannot momentarily identify

SHAK ALE MAN : The struggle that takes place in the night between the urge to urinate and urge to continue sleeping

SHAK LO MUN GRAM : When the urge to continue sleeping takes precedence over all things

SHEAN DORL : Gazing at one's reflection for reasons other than vanity

SHE EAN MIK : Performing prohibited postures before a mirror

SHEM : A slight cold afflicting only one nostril; the thoughts that pass when one shakes hands with a politician

SHUK TACK : The shortening in life-stature a man incurs from a seemingly benevolent machine

SOBI : A reverie lasting less than twenty years on cosmological themes; a nickel

SODI DORL : One machine making way for another; decadence,

particularly in the Cold Continents

SODI IN PIT: Any epithet which does not accurately convey what it intends, such as 'Sober as a judge', 'Silly nit', 'He swims like a fish', 'He's only half-alive', and so on

STAINI RACK NUSVIODON: Experiencing Staini Rack Nuul and then realizing that one must continue in the same outworn fashion because the alternatives are too frightening, or because one is too weak to change; wearing a suit of clothes at which one sees strangers looking askance

STAINI RACK NUUL: Introspection (sometimes prompted by birthdays) that one is not living as one determined to live when one was very young; or, on the other hand, realizing that one is living in a mode decided upon when one was very young and which is now no longer applicable or appropriate

STAIN TOK I: The awareness that one is helplessly living a rôle

STA SODON: The worst feelings which do not even lead to suicide

STA STLAP: The worst feelings which do not even lead to laughter

SU SODA VALKUS: A sudden realization that one's spirit is not pure, overcoming one on Mount Rinvlak (in the Southern Continent)

TI: Civilized aggression

TIG GAG: The creature most like man in the Southern Continent which smiles as it sleeps

TIPY LAP KIN: Laughter that one recognizes though the laugher is unseen; one's own laughter in a crisis

TOK AN: Suddenly divining the nature and imminence of old age in one's thirty-first year

TUAN BOLO: A class of people one meets only at weddings; the pleasure of feeling rather pale

TU KI TOK: Moments of genuine joy captured in a play or charade about joy; the experience of youthful delight in old age

TUZ PAT MAIN (Obs.): The determination to eat one's maternal grandfather

U (Obs.): The amount of time it takes for a lizard to turn into a bird; love

UBI: A girl who lifts her skirts at the very moment you wish she would

UDI KAL : The clothes of the woman one loves

UDI UKAL : The body of the woman one loves

UES WE TEL DA : Love between a male and female politician

UGI SLO GU : The love that needs a little coaxing

UMI RIN TOSIT : The sensation a woman experiences when she does not know how she feels about a man

UMY RIN RU : The new dimensions that take on illusory existence when the body of the loved woman is first revealed

UNIMGAG BU : Love of oneself that passes understanding; a machine's dream

UNK TAK : An out-of-date guide book; the skin shed by the snake that predicts rain

UPANG HOL : Consciousness that one's agonized actions undertaken for love would look rather funny to one's friends

UPANG PLA : Consciousness that while one's agonized actions undertaken for love are on the whole rather funny to oneself, they might even look heroic to one's friends; a play with a cast of three or less

U RI RHI : Two lovers drunk together

USANO NUTO : A novel all about love, written by a computer

USAN I NUT : Dying for love

USAN I ZUN BI : Living for love; a tropical hurricane arriving over the sea, generally at dawn

UZ : Two very large people marrying after the prime of life

UZ TO KARDIN : The realization in childhood that one is the issue of two very large people who married after the prime of life

WE FAAK : A park or a college closed for seemingly good reasons; a city where one wishes one could live

YA GAG : Too much education; a digestive upset during travel

YA GAG LEE : Apologies offered by a hostess for a bad meal; the moment of eclipse

YA GA TUZ : Bad meat; (Obs.) dirty fingernails

YAG ORN : A president

YATUZ PATI (Obs.): The ceremony of eating one's maternal grandfather

YATUZ SHAK SHAK NAPANG HOLI NUN; Lying with one's maternal grandmother; when hens devour their young

YE FLIG TOT : A group of men smiling and congratulating each other

YO FLU GAN : Philosophical thoughts that don't amount to much;

graffiti in a place of worship; childish postponements

YON TORN: A paper tiger; two children with one toy

YON U SAN: The hesitation a boy experiences before first kissing his first girl

YOR KIN BE: A house; a circumlocution; a waterproof hat; the smile of a slightly imperfect wife

YUP PA: A book in which everything is understandable except the author's purpose in writing it; an afternoon sleigh-ride

YUPPA GA: Stomach ache masquerading as eyestrain; a book in which nothing is understandable except the author's purpose in writing it

YUTH MOD: The assumed bonhomie of visitors and strangers

ZO ZO CON: A woman in another field

I, Harad IV, Chief Scribe, declare that this my writing may be shown only to priests of rank within the Orthodox Universal Sacrificial Church and to the Elders Elect of the Council of the Orthodox Universal Sacrificial Church, because here are contained matters concerning the four Vile Heresies that may not be seen or spoken of among the people.

For a Proper Consideration of the newest and vilest heresy, we must look in perspective over the events of history. Accordingly, let us go back to the First Year of our epoch, when the World Darkness was banished by the arrival of the Huge God, our truest, biggest Lord, to whom all honour and terror.

From this present year, 910 HG, it is impossible to recall what the world was like then, but from the few records still surviving, we can gather something of those times and even perform the Mental Contortions necessary to see how events must have looked to the sinners then involved in them.

The world on which the Huge God found himself was full of people and their machines, all of them unprepared for His Visit. There may have been a hundred thousand times more people than now there are.

The Huge God landed in what is now the Sacred Sea, upon which in these days sail some of our most beautiful churches dedicated to His Name. At that time, the region was much less pleasing, being broken up into many states possessed by different nations. This was a system of land tenure practised before our present theories of constant migration and evacuation were formed.

The rear legs of the Huge God stretched far down into Africa – which was then not the island continent it now is – almost touching the Congo River, at the sacred spot marked now by the Sacrificial Church of Basoko-Aketi-Ele, and at the sacred spot marked now by the Temple Church of Aden, obliterating the old port of Aden.

Some of the Huge God's legs stretched above the Sudan and across what was then the Libyan Kingdom, now part of the Sea of Elder Sorrow, while a foot rested in a city called Tunis on what was then the Tunisian shore. These were some of the legs of the Huge God on his left side.

On his right side, his legs blessed and pressed the sands of Saudi Arabia, now called Live Valley, and the foothills of the Caucasus, obliterating the Mount called Ararat in Asia Minor, while the Foremost Leg stretched forward to Russian lands, stamping out immediately the great capital city of Moscow.

The body of the Huge God, resting in repose between his mighty legs, settled mainly over three ancient seas, if the Old Records are to be trusted, called the Sea of Mediterranean, the Red Sea, and the Nile Sea, all of which now form part of the Sacred Sea. He eradicated also with his Great Bulk part of the Black Sea, now called the White Sea, Egypt, Athens, Cyprus, and the Balkan Peninsula as far north as Belgrade, now Holy Belgrade, for above this town towered the Neck of the Huge God on his First Visit to us mortals, just clearing the roofs of the houses.

As for his head, it lifted above the region of mountains that we call Ittaland, which was then named Europe, a populous part of the globe, raised so high that it might easily be seen on a clear day from London, then as now the chief town of the land of the Anglo-French.

It was estimated in those first days that the length of the Huge God was some four and a half thousand miles, from rear to nose, with the eight legs each about nine hundred miles long. Now we profess in our Creed that our Huge God changes shape and length and number of legs according to whether he is Pleased or Angry with man.

In those days, the nature of God was unknown. No preparation had been made for his coming, though some whispers of the millennium were circulating. Accordingly, the speculation on his nature was far from the truth, and often extremely blasphemous.

Here is an extract from the notorious Gersheimer Paper, which contributed much to the events leading up to the First Crusade in 271 HG. We do not know who the Black Gersheimer was, apart from the meaningless fact that he was a Scientific Prophet at somewhere called Cornell or Carnell, evidently a

Church on the American Continent (then a differently shaped territory).

'Aerial surveys suggest that this creature – if one can call it that – which straddles a line along the Red Sea and across south-east Europe, is non-living, at least as we understand life. It may be merely coincidence that it somewhat resembles an eight-footed lizard, so that we do not necessarily have to worry about the thing being malignant, as some tabloids have suggested.'

Not all the vile jargon of that distant day is now understandable, but we believe 'aerial surveys' to refer to the mechanical flying machines which this last generation of the Godless possessed. Black Gersheimer continues:

'If this thing is not live, it may be a piece of galactic debris clinging momentarily to the globe, perhaps like a leaf clinging to a football in the fall. To believe this is not necessarily to alter our scientific concepts of the universe. Whether the thing represents life or not, we don't have to go all superstitious. We must merely remind ourselves that there are many phenomena in the universe as we conceive it in the light of Twentieth Century science which remain unknown to us. However painful this unwanted visitation may be, it is some consolation to think that it will bring us new knowledge – of ourselves, as well as the world outside our little solar system.'

Although terms like 'galactic debris' have lost their meaning, if they ever had one, the general trend of this passage is offensively obvious. An embargo is being set up against the worship of the Huge God, with a heretical God of Science put up in his stead. Only one other passage from this offensive mish-mash need be considered, but it is a vital one for Showing the Attitude of mind of Gersheimer and presumably most of his contemporaries.

'Naturally enough, the peoples of the world, particularly those who are still lingering on the threshold of civilization, are full of fear these days. They see something supernatural in the arrival of this thing, and I believe that every man, if he is honest, will admit to carrying an echo of that fear in his heart. We can only banish it, and can only meet the chaos into which the world is now plunged, if we retain a galactic picture of our situation in our minds. The very hugeness of this thing that now lies plastered loathsomely across our world is cause for terror. But imagine it in proportion. A centipede is sitting on an orange. Or, to pick an analogy that sounds less repulsive, a little gecko, six inches long, is resting momentarily on a plastic globe of the Earth which is two feet in diameter. It is up to us, the human race, with all the technological forces at our disposal, to unite as never before, and blow this thing, this large and stupid object, back into the depths of space from whence it came. Good-night.'

My reasons for repeating this Initial Blasphemy are these: that we can see here in this message from a member of the World Darkness traces of that original sin which – with all our sacrifices, all our hardships, all our crusades – we have not yet stamped out. That is why we are now at the greatest Crisis in the history of the Orthodox Universal Sacrificial Church, and why the time is come for a Fourth Crusade exceeding in scale all others.

The Huge God remained where he was, in what we now refer to as the Sacred Sea Position, for a number of years, absolutely unmoving.

For mankind, this was the great formative period of Belief, marking the establishment of the Universal Church, and characterized by many upheavals. The early priests and prophets suffered much that the Word might go round the World, and the blasphemous sects be destroyed, though the Underground Book of Church Lore suggests that many of them were in fact members of earlier churches who, seeing the light, transferred their allegiances.

The mighty figure of the Huge God was subjected to many puny insults. The Greatest Weapons of that distant age, forces of technical charlatanry, were called Nuclears, and these were dropped on the Huge God – without having any effect, as might be expected. Walls of fire were burnt against him in vain. Our Huge God, to whom all honour and terror, is immune from earthly weakness. His body was Clothed as it were with Metal – here lay the seed of the Second Crusade – but it had not the weakness of metal.

His coming to earth met with immediate Response from nature. The old winds that prevailed were turned aside about his mighty flanks and blew elsewhere. The effect was to cool the centre of Africa, so that the tropical rainforests died and all the creatures in them. In the lands bordering Caspana (then called Persia and Kharkov, say some old accounts), hurricanes of snow fell in a dozen severe winters, blowing far east into India. Elsewhere, all over the world, the coming of the Huge God was felt in the skies, and in freak rainfalls and errant winds, and month-long storms. The oceans also were disturbed, while the great volume of waters displaced by his body poured over the nearby land, killing many thousands of beings and washing ten thousand dead whales into the harbours of Colombo.

The land too joined in the upheaval. While the territory under the Huge God's bulk sank, preparing to receive what would later be the Sacred Sea, the land roundabout rose Up, forming small hills, such as the broken and savage Dolomines that now guard the southern lands of Ittaland. There were earthquakes and new volcanoes and geysers where water never spurted before and plagues of snakes and blazing forests and many wonderful signs that helped the Early Fathers of our faith to convert the ignorant. Everywhere they went, preaching that only in surrender to him lay salvation.

Many Whole Peoples perished at this time of upheaval, such as the Bulgarians, the Egyptians, the Israelites, Moravians, Kurds, Turks, Syrians, Mountain Turks, as well as most of the South Slavs, Georgians, Croats, the sturdy Vlaks, and the Greeks and Cypriotic and Cretan races, together with others whose sins were great and names unrecorded in the annals of the church.

The Huge God departed from the world in the year 89, or some say 90. (This was the First Departure, and is celebrated as such in our Church calendar – though the Catholic Universal Church calls it First Disappearance Day.) He returned in 91, great and aweful be his name.

Little is known of the period when he was absent from our Earth. We get a glimpse into the mind of the people then when we learn that in the main the nations of Earth greatly rejoiced. The natural upheavals continued, since the oceans poured into the great hollow he had made, forming our beloved and holy Sacred Sea. Great Wars broke out across the face of the globe.

His return in 91 halted the wars – a sign of the great peace his presence has brought to his chosen people.

But the inhabitants of the world at That Time were not all of our religion, though prophets moved among them, and many were their blasphemies. In the Black Museum attached to the great basilica of Oma and Yemen is documentary evidence that they tried at this period to communicate with the Huge God by means of their machines. Of course they got no reply – but many men reasoned at this time, in the darkness of their minds, that this was because the God was a Thing, as Black Gersheimer had prophesied.

The Huge God, on this his Second Coming, blessed our earth by settling mainly within the Arctic Circle, or what was then the Arctic Circle, with his body straddling from northern Canada, as it was, over a large peninsula called Alaska, across the Bering Sea and into the northern regions of the Russian lands as far as the River Lena, now the Bay of Lenn. Some of his rear feet broke far into the Arctic Ice, while others of his forefeet entered the Northern Pacific Ocean – but truly to him we are but sand under his feet, and he is indifferent to our mountains or our Climatic Variations.

As for his terrible head, it could be seen reaching far into the stratosphere, gleaming with metal sheen, by all the cities along the northern part of America's seaboard, from such vanished towns as Vancouver, Seattle, Edmonton, Portland, Blanco, Reno, and even San Francisco. It was the energetic and sinful nation that possessed these cities that was now most active against the Huge God. The weight of their ungodly scientific civilization was turned against him, but all they managed to do was blow apart their own coastline.

Meanwhile, other natural changes were taking place. The mass of the Huge God deflected the earth in its daily roll, so that seasons changed and in the prophetic books we read how the great trees brought forth their leaves to cover them in the winter, and lost them in the summer. Bats flew in the daytime and women bore forth hairy children. The melting of the ice caps caused great floods, tidal waves, and poisonous dews, while in one night we hear that the waters of the Deep were moved, so that the tide went out so far from the Malayan Uplands (as they now are) that the continental peninsula of Blestland was formed in a few hours of what had previously been separate Continents or Islands called Singapore, Sumatra, Indonesia, Java, Sydney, and Australia or Austria.

With these powerful signs, our priests could Convert the People, and millions of survivors were speedily enrolled into the Church. This was the First Great Age of the Church, when the word spread across all the ravaged and transformed globe. Our institutions were formed in the next few generations, notably at the various Councils of the New Church (some of which have since proved to be heretical).

We were not established without some difficulty, and many people had to be burned before the rest could feel the faith Burning In Them. But as generations passed, the True Name of the God emerged over a wider and wider area.

Only the Americans still clung largely to their base superstition. Fortified by their science, they refused Grace. So in the year 271 the First Crusade was launched, chiefly against them but also against the Irish, whose heretical views had no benefit of science; the Irish were quickly Eradicated, almost to a man. The Americans were more formidable, but this difficulty served only to draw the people closer and unite the Church further.

This First Crusade was fought over the First Great Heresy of the Church, the heresy claiming that the Huge God was a Thing not a God, as formulated by Black Gersheimer. It was successfully concluded when the leader of the Americans, Lionel Undermeyer, met the Venerable World Emperor-Bishop, Jon II, and agreed that the messengers of the Church should be free to preach unmolested in America. Possibly a harsher decision could have been forced, as some commentators claim, but by this time both sides were suffering severely from plague and famine, the harvest of the world having failed. It was a happy chance that the population of the world was already cut by more than half, or complete starvation would have followed the reorganization of the seasons.

In the churches of the world, the Huge God was asked to give a sign that he had Witnessed the great victory over the American unbelievers. All who opposed this enlightened act were destroyed. He answered the prayers in 297 by moving swiftly forward only a comparatively Small Amount and lying Mainly in the Pacific Ocean, stretching almost as far south as what is now the Antarter, what was then the Tropic of Capricorn, and what had previously been the Equator. Some of his left legs covered the towns along the west American seaboard as far south as

Guadalajara (where the impression of his foot is still marked by the Temple of the Sacred Toe), including some of the towns such as San Francisco already mentioned. We speak of this as the First Shift; it was rightly taken as a striking proof of the Huge God's contempt for America.

This feeling became rife in America also. Purified by famine, plague, gigantic earth tremors, and other natural disorders, the population could now better accept the words of the priests, all becoming converted to a man. Mass pilgrimages were made to see the great body of the Huge God, stretching from one end of their nation to the other. Bolder pilgrims climbed aboard flying aeroplanes and flew over his shoulder, across which savage rain-storms played for a hundred years Without Cease.

Those that were converted became More Extreme than their brethren older in the faith across the other side of the world. No sooner had the American congregations united with ours than they broke away on a point of doctrine at the Council of Dead Tench (322). This date marks the beginning of the Catholic Universal Sacrificial Church. We of the Orthodox persuasion did not enjoy, in those distant days, the harmony with our American brothers that we do now.

The doctrinal point on which the churches split apart was, as is well known, the question of whether humanity should wear clothes that imitated the metallic sheen of the Huge God. It was claimed that this was setting up man in God's Image; but it was a calculated slur on the Orthodox Universal priests, who wore plastic or metal garments in honour of their maker.

This developed into the Second Great Heresy. As this long and confused period has been amply dealt with elsewhere, we may pass over it lightly here, mentioning merely that the quarrel reached its climax in the Second Crusade, which the American Catholic Universals launched against us in 450. Because they still had a large preponderance of machines, they were able to force their point, to sack various monasteries along the edge of the Sacred Sea, to defile our women, and to retire home in glory.

Since that time, everyone in the world has worn only garments of wool or fur. All who opposed this enlightened act were destroyed.

It would be wrong to emphasize too much the struggles of the past. All this while, the majority of people were peacefully about their worship, being sacrificed regularly, and praying every sunset and sunrise (whenever they might occur) that the Huge God would leave our world, since we were not worthy of him.

The Second Crusade left a trail of troubles in its wake; the next fifty years were, on the whole, not happy ones. The American armies returned home to find that the heavy pressure upon their western seaboard had opened up a number of volcanoes along their biggest mountain range, the Rockies. Their country was covered in fire and lava, and their air filled with stinking ash.

Rightly, they accepted this as a sign that their conduct left much to be desired in the eyes of the Huge God (for though it has never been proved that he has eyes, he surely Sees Us). Since the rest of the world had not been Visited with punishment on quite this scale, they correctly divined that their sin was that they still clung to technology and the weapons of technology against the wishes of God.

With their faith strong within them, every last instrument of science, from the Nuclears of the Canopeners, was destroyed, and a hundred thousand virgins of the persuasion were dropped into suitable volcanoes as propitation. All who opposed these enlightened acts were destroyed, and some ceremonially eaten.

We of the Orthodox Universal faith applauded our brothers' whole-hearted action. Yet we could not be sure they had purged themselves enough. Now that they owned no weapons and we still had some, it was clear we could help them in their purgation. Accordingly, a mighty armada of one hundred and sixty-six wooden ships sailed across to America, to help them suffer for the faith – and incidentally to get back some of our loot. This was the Third Crusade of 482, under Jon the Chubby.

While the two opposed armies were engaged in battle outside New York, the Second Shift took place. It lasted only a matter of five minutes.

In that time, the Huge God turned to his left flank, crawled across the centre of what was then the North American continent, crossed the Atlantic as if it were a puddle, moved over Africa, and came to rest in the south Indian Ocean, demolishing Madagaska with one rear foot. Night fell Everywhere on Earth.

When dawn came, there could hardly have been a single man who did not believe in the power and wisdom of the Huge God, to whose name belongs all Terror and Might. Unhappily, among those who were unable to believe were the contesting armies, who were one and all swept under a Wave of Earth and Rock as the God passed.

In the ensuing chaos, only one note of sanity prevailed – the sanity of the Church. The Church established as the Third Great Heresy the idea that any machines were permissible to man against the wishes of God. There was some doctrinal squabble as to whether books counted as machines. It was decided they did, just to be on the safe side. From then on, all men were free to do nothing but labour in the fields and worship, and pray to the Huge God to remove himself to a world more worthy of his might. At the same time, the rate of sacrifices was stepped up, and the Slow-Burning Method was introduced (499).

Now followed the great Peace, which lasted till 900. In all this time, the Huge God never moved; it has been truly said that the centuries are but seconds in his sight. Perhaps mankind has never known such a long peace, four hundred years of it – a peace that existed in his heart if not outside it, because the world was naturally in Some Disorder. The great force of the Huge God's progress halfway across the world had altered the progression of day and night to a considerable extent; some legends claim that, before the Second Shift, the sun used to rise in the east and set in the west – the very opposite of the natural order of things we know.

Gradually, this peaceful period saw some re-establishment of order of the seasons, and some cessation of the floods, showers of blood, hailstorms, earthquakes, deluges of icicles, apparitions of comets, volcanic eruptions, miasmic fogs, destructive winds, blights, plagues of wolves and dragons, tidal waves, year-long thunderstorms, lashing rains, and sundry other scourges of which the scriptures of this period speak so eloquently. The Fathers of the Church, retiring to the comparative safety of the inland seas and sunny meadows of Gobiland in Mongolia, established a new orthodoxy, well-calculated in its rigour of prayer and human burnt-offering to incite the Huge God to leave our poor wretched world for a better and more substantial one.

So the story comes almost to the present – to the year 900, only a decade past as your scribe writes. In that year, the Huge

God left our earth!

Recall, if you will, that the First Departure in 89 lasted only twenty months. Yet the Huge God has been gone from us already half that number of years! We need him Back – we cannot live without him, as we should have realized Long Ago had we not blasphemed in our hearts!

On his going, he propelled our humble globe on such a course that we are doomed to deepest winter all the year; the sun is far away and shrunken; the seas Freeze half the year; icebergs march across our fields; at midday, it is too dark to read without a rush light. Woe is us!

Yet we deserve everything we get. This is a just punishment, for throughout all the centuries of our epoch, when our kind was so relatively happy and undisturbed, we prayed like fools that the Huge God would leave us.

I ask all the Elders Elect of the Council to brand those prayers as the Fourth and Greatest Heresy, and to declare that henceforth all men's efforts be devoted to calling on the Huge God to return to us at once.

I ask also that the sacrifice rate be stepped up again. It is useless to skimp things just because we are running out of women.

I ask also that a Fourth Crusade be launched – fast, before the air starts to freeze in our nostrils!

I

Under the impact of sunlight, the ocean seemed to burn. Out of the confusion of its flames and its long breakers, an old motor vessel was emerging, engine thudding as it headed for the narrow channel among the coral reefs. Two or three pairs of eyes watched it from the shore, one pair protected behind dark glasses from the glare beyond.

The *Kraken* shut off its engines. As it slid between the pincers of coral, it let off a double blast from its siren. Minutes later, it lost all forward momentum, and an anchor rattled down on to the collapsed coral bed, clearly visible under the water. Then it was rubbing its paintless hull against the landing stage.

The landing stage, running out from the shore over the shallow water, creaked and swayed. As it and the ship became one unit, and a Negro in a greasy nautical cap jumped down from the deck to secure the mooring lines, a woman detached herself from the shade of the coconut palms that formed a crest to the first rise of the beach. She came slowly forward, almost cautiously, dangling her sunglasses now from a hand held at shoulder level. She came down on to the landing stage, her sandals creaking and tapping over the slats.

The motor vessel had its faded green canopy up, protecting part of the fore-deck from the annihilating sun. A bearded man stuck his head out of the side of the rail, emerging suddenly from the shadow of the canvas. He wore nothing but a pair of old jeans, rolled high up his calf – jeans, and a pair of steel-rimmed spectacles; his body was tanned brown. He was ambiguously in his mid-forties, a long-faced man called Clement Yale. He was coming home.

Smiling at the woman, he jumped down on to the landing stage. For a moment they stood regarding each other. He looked at the line that now divided her brow, at the slight wrinkles by the corners of her eyes, at the fold that increasingly encompassed her full mouth. He saw that she had applied lipstick and powder for this great event of his return. He was moved by

113

what he saw; she was still beautiful – and in that phrase, 'still beautiful', was the melancholy echo of another thought. She tires, she tires, although her race is not half-run!

'Caterina!' he said.

As they went into each other's arms, he thought. But perhaps, perhaps it could now be arranged that she would live – well, let's be conservative and say ... say six or seven hundred years....

After a minute, they broke apart. The sweat from his torso had marked her dress. He said, 'I must help them unload a few essentials, darling, then I'll be with you. Where's Philip? He's still here, isn't he?'

'He's somewhere around,' she said, making a vague gesture at the backdrop of palms, their house, and the scrub-clad cliff behind that – the only high ground on Kalpeni. She put the sunglasses on again, and Yale turned back to the ship.

She watched him move sparely, recalling that laconic and individual way he had of ordering both his sentences and his limbs. He set about directing the eight crew quietly, joking with Louis, the fat creole cook from Mauritius, supervising the removal of his electron microscope. Gradually, a small pile of boxes and trunks appeared on the wooden quay. Once he looked round to see if Philip was about, but the boy was not to be seen.

She moved back to the shore as the men began to shoulder their loads. Without looking round, she climbed the board walk over the sand, and went into the house.

Most of the baggage from the ship was taken into the laboratory next door, or the store adjoining it. Yale brought up the rear, carrying a hutch made from old orange boxes. Between the bars of the hutch, two young Adelie penguins peered, croaking to each other.

He walked through into the house by the back door. It was a simple one-storey structure, built of chunks of coral and thatched in the native manner, or the native manner before the Madrassis had started importing corrugated iron to the atolls.

'You'd like a beer, darling,' she said, stroking his arm.

'Can't you rustle some up for the boys? Where's Philip?'

'I said I don't know.'

'He must have heard the ship's siren.'

'I'll get some beer.'

She went through into the kitchen where Joe, the boy, was lounging at the door. Yale looked round the cool familiar living-room at the paperbacks propped up with seashells, the rug they had bought in Bombay on the way out here, the world map, and the oil portrait of Caterina hanging on the walls. It had been months since he had been home – well, it really was home, though in fact it was only a fisheries research station to which they had been posted. Caterina was here, so it must be home, but they could now think about getting back to the U.K. The research stint was over, the tour of duty done. It would be better for Philip if they went home to roost, at least temporarily, while he was still at university. Yale went to the front door and looked along the length of the island.

Kalpeni was shaped like an old-fashioned beer bottle opener, the top bar of which had been broken by sea action to admit small boats into the lagoon. Along the shaft of the island grew palms. Right at the far end lay the tiny native settlement, a few ugly huts, not visible from here because of intervening higher ground.

'Yes, I'm home,' he said to himself. Along with his happiness ran a thread of worry, as he wondered how he'd ever face the gloom of the Northern European climate.

He saw his wife through the window talking to the crew of the trawler, watched their faces and drew pleasure from their pleasure in looking at and talking to a pretty woman again. Joe trotted behind her with a tray full of beers. He went out and joined them, sat on the bench beside them and enjoyed the beer.

When he had the chance, he said to Caterina, 'Let's go and find Philip.'

'You go, darling. I'll stay and talk to the men.'

'Come with me.'

'Philip will turn up. There's no hurry.'

'I've something terribly important to tell you.'

She looked anxious. 'What sort of thing?'

'I'll tell you this evening.'

'About Philip?'

'No, of course not. Is anything the matter with Philip?'

'He wants to be a writer.'

Yale laughed. 'It isn't long since he wanted to be a moon pilot, is it? Has he grown very much?'

'He's practically an adult. He's serious about being a writer.'

'How've you been, darling? You haven't been too bored? Where's Fraulein Reise, by the way?'

Caterina retreated behind her dark glasses and looked towards the low horizon. 'She got bored. She went home. I'll tell you later.' She laughed awkwardly. 'We've got so much to tell each other, Clem. How was the Antarctic?'

'Oh – marvellous! You should have been with us, Cat! Here it's a world of coral and sea – there it's ice and sea. You can't imagine it. It's clean. All the time I was there, I was in a state of excitement. It's like Kalpeni – it will always belong to itself, never to man.'

When the crew were moving back to the ship, he put on a pair of canvas shoes and strolled out towards the native huts to look for his son Philip.

Among the shanties, nothing moved. Just clear of the long breakers, a row of fishing boats lay on the sand. An old woman sat against the elephant-grey bole of a palm, watching an array of jewfish drying before her, too idle to brush the flies away from her eyelids. Nothing stirred but the unending Indian Ocean. Even the cloud over distant Karavatti was anchored there. From the largest hut, which served also as a store, came the thin music of a radio and a woman singing.

> *Happiness, oh Happiness,*
> *It's what you are, it's not Progress.*

The same, Yale thought to himself dryly, applied to laziness. These people had the good life here, or their version of it. They wanted to do nothing, and their wish was almost entirely fulfilled. Caterina also liked the life. She could enjoy looking at the vacant horizon day after day; HE had always to be doing. You had to accept that people differed – but he had always accepted that, taken pleasure in it.

He ducked his head and went into the big hut. A genial and plump young Madrassi, all oiled and black and shining, sat behind his counter picking his teeth. His name was over the door, painted painfully on a board in English and Sanscrit, 'V. K. Vandranasis'. He rose and shook hands with Yale.

'You are glad to get back from the South Pole, I presume?'

'Pretty glad, Vandranasis.'

'Without doubt the South Pole is cold even in this warm weather?'

'Yes, but we've been on the move, you know – covered practically ten thousand nautical miles. We didn't simply sit on the Pole and freeze! How's life with you? Making your fortune?'

'Now, now, Mr. Yale, on Kalpeni are no fortunes to be made. That you surely know!' He beamed with pleasure at Yale's joke. 'But life is not too bad here. Suddenly you know we got a swarm of fish here, more than the men can catch. Kalpeni never before got so many fish!'

'What sort of fish? Jewfish?'

'Yes, yes, many many jewfish. Other fish not so plenty, but the jewfish are now in their millions.'

'And the whales still come?'

'Yes, yes, when it is full moon the big whales are coming.'

'I thought I saw their carcasses up by the old fort.'

'That is perfectly correct. Five carcasses. The last one last month and one the month before at the time of the full moon. I think maybe they come to eat the jewfish.'

'That can't be. The whales started visiting the Laccadives before we had a glut of jewfish. In any case, blue whales don't eat jewfish.'

V. K. Vandranasis put his head cutely on one side and said, 'Many strange things happen you science-wallahs and learned men don't know. There's always plenty change happening in the old world, don't you know? Maybe this year the blue whales newly are learning to appreciate eating the jewfish. At least, that is my theory.'

Just to keep the man in business, Yale bought a bottle of raspberryade and drank the warm scarlet liquid as they chatted. The storekeeper was happy to give him the gossip of the island, which had about as much flavour to it as the sugary mess Yale was drinking. In the end, Yale had to cut him short by asking if he had seen Philip; but Philip had not been down this end of the island for a day or two, it appeared. Yale thanked him, and started back along the strip of beach, past the old woman still motionless before her drying fish.

He wanted to get back and think about the jewfish. The

months-long survey of ocean currents he had just completed, which had been backed by the British Ministry of Fisheries and Agriculture and the Smithsonian Oceanic Research Institute under the aegis of the World Waters Organization, had been inspired by a glut of fish – in this case a superabundance of herring in the over-fished waters of the Baltic, which had begun ten years ago and continued ever since. That superabundance was spreading slowly to the herring banks of the North Sea; in the last two years, those once-vast reservoirs of fish had been yielding and even surpassing their old abundance. He knew, too, from his Antarctic expedition, that the Adelie penguins were also greatly on the increase. And there would be other creatures, also proliferating, unrecorded as yet.

All these apparently random increases in animal population seemed not to have been made at the expense of any other animal – though obviously that state of affairs would not be maintained if the numbers multiplied to really abnormal proportions.

It was a coincidence that these increases came at a time when the human population explosion had tailed off. Indeed, the explosion had been more of a dread myth than an actuality; now it had turned into a phantom or might-have-been, rather like the danger of uncontained nuclear war, which had also vanished in this last decade of the old twentieth century. Man had not been able voluntarily to curtail his reproductive rate to any statistically significant extent, but the mere fact of overcrowding with all its attendant physical discomforts and anti-familial pressures, and with its psychic pressures of neurosis, sexual aberration and sterility operating exactly in the areas previously most fecund, had proved dynamic enough to level off the accelerating birth spiral in the dense population centres. One result of this was a time of tranquillity in international affairs such as the world had hardly known throughout the rest of the century.

It was curious to think of such matters on Kalpeni. The Laccadives lay awash in ocean and sun; their lazy peoples lived on a diet of dry fish and coconut, exporting nothing but dry fish and copra; they were remote from the grave issues of the century – of any century. And yet, Yale reminded himself, misquoting Donne, no island is an island. Already these shores were lapped by the waves of a new and mysterious change that was flooding the world for better or worse – a change over which man had absolutely no command, any more than he could command the flight of the lonely albatross through the air above the southern oceans.

II

Caterina came out of the coral-built house to meet her husband.

'Philip's home, Clem!' she said, taking his hand.

'Why the anxiety?' he asked, then saw his son emerge from the shade, ducking slightly to avoid the lintel of the door. He came forward and put his hand out to his father. As they shook hands, Philip smiling and blushing, Yale saw he had indeed grown adult.

This son by his first marriage – Yale had married Caterina only three and a half years ago – looked much as Yale himself had done at seventeen, with his fair hair clipped short and a long mobile face that too easily expressed the state of mind of its owner.

'Good to see you again. Come on in and have a beer with me,' Yale said. 'I'm glad the *Kraken* got back here before you had to leave for England.'

'Well, I wanted to speak to you about that, Father. I think I'd better go home on the *Kraken* – I mean, get a lift in it to Aden, and fly home from there.'

'No! They sail tomorrow, Phil! I shall see so little of you. You don't have to leave so soon, surely?'

Philip looked away, then said as he sat down at the table opposite his father, 'Nobody asked you to be away the best part of a year.'

The answer caught Yale unexpectedly. He said, 'Don't think I haven't missed you and Cat.'

'That doesn't answer the question, does it?'

'Phil, you didn't ask me a question. I'm sorry I was away so long, but the job had to be done. I hoped you'd be able to stay here a bit longer, so that we could see more of each other. Why have you got to go all of a sudden?'

The boy took the beer that Caterina had brought, raised his glass to her as she sat down between them, and took a long drink. Then he said, 'I have to work, Father. I take finals next year.'

'You're going to stay with your mother in the U.K.?'

'She's in Cannes or somewhere with one of her rich boyfriends. I'm going to stay in Oxford with a friend and study.'

'A girl friend, Phil?'

The attempt at teasing did not come off. He repeated sullenly, 'A friend.'

Silence overcame them. Caterina saw they were both looking at her neat brown hands, which lay before her on the table. She drew them on to her lap and said, 'Well, let's all three of us go and have a swim in the lagoon, the way we used to.'

The two men rose, but without enthusiasm, not liking to refuse.

They changed into their swim things. Excitement and pleasure buoyed Yale as he saw his wife in a bikini again. Her body was as attractive as ever, and browner, her thighs not an ounce too heavy, her breasts firm. She grinned naughtily at him as if guessing his thoughts and took his hand in hers. As they went down to the landing stage, carrying flippers and goggles and snorkels, Yale said, 'Where were you hiding out when the *Kraken* arrived, Phil?'

'I was in the fort, and I was not hiding.'

'I was only asking. Cat says you're taking up writing.'

'Oh, does she?'

'What are you writing? Fiction? Poetry?'

'I suppose you'd call it fiction.'

'What would you call it?'

'Oh, for Christ's sake, stop examining me, can't you? I'm not a bloody kid any more, you know!'

'Sounds as if I came back on the wrong day!'

'Yes, you did, if you want to know! You divorced mother and then you went chasing after Cat and married her – why don't you look after her if you want her?'

He flung his equipment down, took a run along the wooden platform, and made a fast shallow dive into the blue waters. Yale looked at Caterina, but she avoided his stare.

'He sounds as if he's jealous! Have you been getting a lot of this sort of thing?'

'He's at the moody stage. You must leave him alone. Don't

annoy him.'

'I've hardly spoken to him.'

'Don't oppose his going away tomorrow if he's set on it.'

'You two have been quarrelling over something, haven't you?'

He was looking down at her. She was sitting on the platform, putting on her flippers. As he looked down at the well between her breasts, love overcame him again. They must go back to London, and Cat must start a baby, for her sake; you could sacrifice too much just for the sake of sunlight; civilized behaviour could be defined as a readiness to submit to increased doses of artificial light and heat; maybe there was a direct relationship between the ever-growing world demand for power and a bolstering of the social contract. His moment's speculation was checked by her reply.

'On the contrary, we got on very well when you weren't here.'

Something in her tone made him stand where he was, looking after her as she swam towards her stepson, sporting in the middle of the lagoon beyond the *Kraken*. Slowly, he pulled down his goggles and launched himself after her.

The swim did them all good. After what Vandranasis had said, Yale was not surprised to find jewfish in the lagoon, although they generally stayed on the outer side of the atoll. There was one fat old fellow in particular, over six feet long and half-inclined to set up a leering and contemptuous friendship that made Yale wish he had brought the harpoon gun.

When he had had enough, Yale swam over to the north-west side of the lagoon, below the old Portuguese fort, and lay in the gritty coral sand. The others came and joined him in a few minutes.

'This is the life,' he said, putting an arm round Caterina. 'Some of our so-called experts explain all of life in terms of our power drives, others see everything explicable in terms of God's purpose; for another, it's all a matter of glands, or for another it all boils down to a question of sublimated incest-wishes. But for me, I see life as a quest for sunlight.'

He caught his wife's strained look.

'What's the matter? Don't you agree?'

'I – no, Clem, I – well, I suppose I have other goals.'

'What?'

When she didn't answer, he said to Philip, 'What are your

goals in life, young man?'

'Why do you always ask such boring questions? I just live. I don't intellectualize all the time.'

'Why did Fraulein Reise go home? Was it because you were as discourteous to her as you are to me?'

'Oh, go to . . .' He got up, roughly pulled on his mask, and flung himself back in the water, striking out violently for the far beach. Yale stood up, kicked off his flippers, and trod up the beach, ignoring the sharp bite of the coral sand. Over the top of the bank, scraggy grass grew, and then the slope tilted down towards the reef and the long barrier of ocean. Here the whales lay rotting, half out of water, flesh that was now something too terrible to count any more as flesh. Fortunately the south-west trades kept the stench away from the other side of the island; sniffing it now, Yale recalled that this scent of corruption had trailed far across the sea to the *Kraken*, as if all Kalpeni were the throne of some awful and immeasurable crime. He thought of that now, as he tried to control his anger against his son.

That evening, they gave supper to the men of the little trawler. It was a genial farewell meal, but it broke up early and afterwards Yale, Philip, and Caterina sat on the veranda, taking a final drink and looking across to the lights of the *Kraken* in the lagoon. Philip seemed to have completely recovered from his earlier sulkiness and was talking cheerfully, burbling on about life at the university until finally Caterina interrupted him.

'I've heard enough about Oxford over the past few weeks. How about hearing about the Antarctic from Clem?'

'It all sounds a gloomy dump to me.'

'It has its vile moments and its good moments,' Clem said, 'which I suppose could be claimed for Oxford too. Take these penguins I've brought back. The conditions in which their species mates are death to man – perhaps minus thirty degrees Fahrenheit and with a howling snowstorm moving over them at something like eighty miles an hour. You'd literally freeze solid in that sort of weather, yet the penguins regard it as ideal for courting.'

'More fool them!'

'They have their reasons. At certain times of year, Antarctica is swimming with food, the richest place in the world. Oh, you'll have to go there one day, Philip. Great doses of daylight in the summer! It's – well, it's another planet down there, and far more undiscovered than the moon. Do you realize that more people have set foot on the moon than have ever ventured into the Antarctic?'

The reasons for the *Kraken*'s sailing into those far south waters had been purely scientific. The newly established World Waters Organization, with its headquarters in a glittering new skyscraper on the Bay of Naples, had inaugurated a five-year study of oceans, and the rusty old *Kraken* was an inglorious part of the Anglo-American contribution. Equipped with Davis-Swallows and other modern oceanographic instrumentation, it had been at work for many months charting the currents of the Atlantic. During that time, Clement Yale had done an unexpected piece of detective work.

'I told you this morning I had something important to say. I'd better get it off my chest now. You know what a copepod is, Cat?'

'I've heard you speak of them. They're fish, aren't they?'

'They're crustaceans living among the plankton, and a vital link in the food chain of oceans. It's been computed that there may be more individual copepods than there are individuals in all other multi-celled animal classes combined – all human beings, fish, oysters, monkeys, dogs, and so on – the lot. A copepod is about the size of a rice grain. Some genera eat half their own weight of food – mainly diatoms – in a day. The world's champion pig never managed that. The rate at which this little sliver of life ingests and reproduces might well stand as a symbol of the fecundity of old Earth.

'It might stand, too, for the way in which all life is linked all round the globe. The copepods feed on the smallest living particles in the ocean, and are eaten by some of the largest, in particular the whale shark and the basking shark and various whales. Several sea-going birds like a bit of copepod in their diet too.

'The different genera of copepod infest different lanes and levels in the multi-dimensional world of the ocean. We followed one genus for thousands of miles while we were tracking one particular ocean current.'

'Oh – oh, I thought he was edging on to his favourite topic!'

Philip said.

'Get you father another drink and don't cheek him. The complex of ocean flow is as necessary to human life as the circulation of the blood. The one as much as the other is the stream of existence, bearing us all forward willy-nilly. On the *Kraken*, we were interested in one part of that stream in particular, a current of whose existence oceanographers were aware in theory for some time. Now we have charted it exactly, and named it.

'I'll tell you the name of this current in a minute. It'll amuse you, Cat. The current starts lazily in the Tyrrhenian Sea, which is the name of the bit of the Mediterranean between Sardinia, Sicily, and Italy. We've swum in it more than once off Sorento, Cat, but to us it was just "the Med". Anyhow, the evaporation rate is high there, and the extra salty water sinks and spills out eventually into the Atlantic, of which the Med is just a landlocked arm.

'The current sinks further and deflects south. We could follow it quite easily with salinity gauges and flow-rate recorders and so on. It divides, but the particular stream we were interested in remains remarkably homogeneous and comprises a narrow ribbon of water moving at a rate of about three miles a day. In the Atlantic, it is sandwiched between two other currents moving in the opposite direction, currents that have been known for some years as the Antarctic Intermediate Water and the Antarctic Bottom Water. Both these north-flowing streams are considerable masses of water – main arteries, you could call them. The Bottom Water is highly saline and icy cold.

'We followed our current right across the Equator and down into southern latitudes, into the cold waters of the Southern Ocean. It is eventually forced to the surface, fanning out as it rises, from the Weddell to the Mackenzie Sea, along the Antarctic coast. In this warmer water, during the short polar summer, the copepods and other small fry proliferate. Another little crustacean, the euphaustids or "krill", turns the seas cinnamon, so many of them pack the waters. The *Kraken* often rode on a pink sea. While they're feeding on diatoms, the whales are feeding on them.'

'Nature's so horrible!' Caterina said.

Yale smiled at her. 'Maybe, but there's nothing else *but* nature! Anyhow, we were very proud of our current for making such a long journey. Do you know what we have called it? We've named it in honour of the Director of the World Waters Organization. It is to be known as the Devlin Current, after Theodore Devlin, the great marine ecologist and your first husband.'

Caterina looked most striking when she was angry. Reaching for a cigarette from the sandalwood box on the table, she said, 'I suppose that is your idea of a joke!'

'It's an irony perhaps. But it's only fitting, don't you know. Give the devil his due! Devlin's a great man, more important than I shall ever be.'

'Clem, you know how he treated me!'

'Of course I do. Because of that treatment, I was lucky enough to get you. I hold no malice for the man. After all, he was once a friend of mine.'

'No, he wasn't. Theo has no friends, only expediencies. After my five years with him I should know him better than you.'

'You could be prejudiced.' He smiled, rather enjoying her annoyance.

She threw the cigarette at him and jumped up. 'You're crazy, Clem! You drive me mad! Why don't you sometimes get your back up at someone? You're always so damned level-tempered. Why can't you hate someone, ever? Theo in particular! Why couldn't you hate Theo for my sake?'

He stood up too. 'I love you when you're trying to be a bitch.'

She smacked him across the face, sending his spectacles flying, and stamped out of the room. Philip did not move. Yale went over to the nearest cane chair and picked his spectacles up from the seat; they were not broken. As he put them on again, he said, 'I hope these scenes don't embarrass you too much, Phil. We all need safety valves for our emotions, women in particular. Caterina's marvellous, isn't she? Don't you think? You did get on well with her, didn't you?'

Philip flushed a slow red. 'I'll leave you to your capers. I have to go and pack.'

As he turned, Yale caught his arm. 'You don't have to go. You are almost adult. You must face violent emotions. You never could as a child – but they're as natural as storms at sea.'

'Child! You're the child, Father! You think you're so poised and understanding, don't you? But you've never understood how people feel!'

He pulled himself away. Yale was left standing in the room alone. '*Explain* and I'd understand,' he said aloud.

III

When he walked into the bedroom, Caterina was sitting dejectedly on her bed, barefoot, with her feet resting on the stone floor. She looked up at him intently, with something of the inscrutable stare of a cat.

'I drank too much tonight, darling. You know beer doesn't agree with me. I'm sorry!'

Yale went over to her, pulled the rug under her feet, and knelt beside her. 'You horrible alcoholic! Come and help me feed the penguins before we turn in. Philip's gone to bed, I think.'

'Say you've forgiven me.'

'Oh, Christ, let's not have *that*, my sweet Cat! You can see I have forgiven you.'

'Say it then, say it!'

He thought to himself, 'Phil's entirely right, I don't understand anyone. I don't even understand myself. It's true I have forgiven Cat; why then should I be reluctant to say so because she insists I say so? Maybe it was because I thought there was so little to forgive. Well, what's a man's dignity beside a woman's need?' And he said it.

Outside, the waves made slumberous noises along the reef, a sound of continuous content. The island looked so low by night that it seemed a wonder the sea did not sweep over it. Not a light showed anywhere except for the lamp on the *Kraken*'s mast.

The two penguins were in one of the permanent cages at the rear of the lab. They stood with their beaks tucked under their flippers, asleep, and did not alter their position when the lights came on.

She put an arm round his waist. 'Sorry I flew off the handle. I suppose we ought to have congratulated you? I mean, I suppose this current is rather a big discovery, isn't it?'

'It's certainly a *long* discovery – nine and a half thousand miles long.'

'Oh, be serious, darling. You're underplaying what you've done as usual, aren't you?'

'Oh, terribly! I may get a knighthood any day. Anyhow, we'll have to fly to London in a week to receive some sort of applause, and I'll have to make a fuller report than I have done so far. In fact there is another discovery that I've only communicated to one other person as yet which makes the discovery of Devlin's Current seem nothing, a discovery that could affect every one of us.'

'What do you mean?'

'It's late and we're both tired. You shall hear about it in the morning.'

'Can't you tell me now, while you're feeding the birds?'

'They're okay. I just wanted to check on them. They'll feed better in the morning.' He looked speculatively at her.

'I am a greedy man, Cat, though I try to hide it. I want life, I'd like to share life with you for a thousand years, I'd like to roam the Earth for a thousand years – with or without a knighthood! That may be possible.'

They stood looking for each other, feeling for the neural currents that flowed between them, relaxed enough after their tiff to feel that they were no longer two entirely separate organisms.

'There's a new infection in the world's blood-stream,' he said. 'It could bring a sort of illness that we could call longevity. It was first isolated in the herring schools in the Baltic a decade ago. It's a virus. Cat – you understand how we traced the Devlin Current, don't you? We had deep trawls and sonar devices and special floats that sink to predetermined water densities, so that we could trace the particular salinity and temperature and speed of our current all the way. We could also check the plankton content. We found that the copepods carried a particular virus that I could identify as a form of the Baltic virus – it's a highly characteristic form. We don't know where the virus came from originally. The Russians think it was brought to Earth encased in a tektite, or by meteoritic dust, so that it may be extra-terrestrial in origin —'

'Clem, please, all this is beyond me! What does this virus *do*? It lengthens life, you say?'

'In certain cases. In certain genera.'

'In men and women?'

'No. Not yet. Not as far as I know.' He gestured towards the equipment on the lab bench. 'I'll show you what it looks like when I get the electron microscope set up. The virus is very small, about twenty millimicrons long. Once it finds a host it can use, it spreads rapidly through the cell tissue, where its action appears to be the destruction of anything threatening the life of the cell. In fact, it is a cell repairer, and a very effective one at that. You see what that means! Any life form infected with it is inclined to live for ever. The Baltic virus will even rebuild cells completely where it finds a really suitable host. So far, it seems to have found only two such hosts, both sea-going, one fish, one mammal, the herring and the blue whale. In the copepods it is merely latent.'

He could see that Caterina was trembling. She said, 'You mean that all herring and blue whales are – immortal?'

'Potentially so, if they've caught the infection, yes. Of course, the herrings get eaten, but the ones that don't, go on reproducing year after year with unimpaired powers. None of the animals that eat the herring appear to catch the infection. In other words, the virus cannot sustain itself in them. It's an irony that this minute germ holds the secret of eternal life, yet is itself threatened constantly with extinction.'

'But people —'

'People don't come into it yet. The copepods we traced along our current were infected with the Baltic virus. They surfaced in the Antarctic. That was one of the discoveries I made – that there is another species that can be infected. The Adelie penguins have it too. They just don't die from natural causes any more. These two birds here are virtually immortal.'

She stood looking at them through the mesh of the cage. The penguins perched on the edge of their tank, their comical feet gripping its tiled lip. They had awakened without removing their beaks from their wings, and now regarded the woman with bright and unwinking eyes.

'Clem – it's funny, generations of men have dreamed of immortality. But they never thought it would come to penguins. ... I suppose that's what you'd call an irony! Is there any way we can infect ourselves from these birds?'

He laughed. 'It's not as easy as picking up psittacosis from a parrot. But it may be that laboratory research will find a means of infecting human beings with this disease. Before that happens, there's another question we ought to ask ourselves.'

'How do you mean?'

'Isn't there a moral question first? Are we capable, either as a species or as individuals, of living fruitfully for a thousand years? Do we deserve it?'

'Do you think herrings deserve it more than we do?'

'They cause less damage than man.'

'Try telling that to your copepods!'

This time he laughed with genuine pleasure, enjoying one of the rare occasions when he considered she answered him back wittily.

'It's interesting the way copepods carry the virus in a latent form all the way down from the Med to the Antarctic without becoming infected themselves. Of course, there must be a connecting link between the Baltic and the Med, but we haven't found it yet.'

'Could it be another current?'

'Don't think so. We just don't know. Meanwhile, the ecology of Earth is slowly being turned upside down. Up till now, it has just meant a pleasant glut of food and the survival of whales that were on the threshold of extinction, but it may lead in time to famines and other unpleasant natural upheavals.'

Caterina was less interested in that aspect. 'Meanwhile, you are going to see if the virus can be implanted in us?'

'That could be very dangerous. Besides, it's not my field.'

'You're not just going to let it slide?'

'No. I've kept the whole matter secret, even from the others on the *Kraken*. I've communicated the problem to only one other person. You'll hate me for this, Cat, but this thing is far too important to let personalities enter the situation. I sent a coded report to Theo Devlin at the WWO in Naples. I shall drop in to see him on our way back to London.'

Suddenly her face looked tired and aged. 'You're either a saint or you're raving mad,' she said.

The penguins watched without moving as the two humans left the room. Long after lights went out, they shut their eyes and returned to sleep.

Dawn next morning set the sky afire with a more than Wagnerian splendour, revealing the first sluggish activity on the *Kraken*, and mingling with the smell of preserved eggs frying in the galley. In four or five days, the crew would be back at their base in Aden, enjoying fresh and varied food again.

Philip was also astir early. He had slept naked between the sheets and did nothing more in the way of dressing than slipping on a pair of swimming trunks. He walked round the back of the house and looked into his father's bedroom window. Yale and Cat both slumbered peacefully together in her bed. He turned away, his face distorted, and made his way falteringly down to the lagoon for a last swim. A short while later, Joe, the Negrito house boy, was bustling round the house, getting the breakfast and singing a song about the coolness of the hour.

As the day grew hotter, the bustle of preparation for departure increased. Yale and his wife were invited aboard the trawler for a farewell lunch, which was eaten under the deck canopy. Although Yale tried to talk to Philip, his son had retired behind his morose mood and would not be drawn; Yale comforted himself by reflecting that they would meet again in the U.K. in a very few days.

The ship sailed shortly after noon, sounding its siren when it moved through the narrow mouth of the reef as it had done when it entered. Yale and Cat waved for a while from the shade of the palms, and then turned away.

'Poor Philip! I hope his holiday did him good. That troubled adolescent phase is hard to deal with. I went through just the same thing, I remember!'

'Did you, Clem? I doubt it.' She looked about her desperately, at her husband's gentle face, at the harsh sea on which the trawler was still clearly visible, up at the heavy leaves of palm above them. In none of these elements, it seemed, could she find help. She burst out, 'Clem, I can't keep it a secret, I must tell you now, I don't know what you'll say or what it'll do to you, but, these last few weeks, Philip and I have been lovers!'

He looked at her in a puzzled way, eyes narrow behind his lenses, as if he could not understand the expression she had used.

'That's why he went off the way he did! He couldn't bear to be around when you were. He begged me never to tell you....

He. . . . Clem, it was all my fault, I should have known better.'
She paused and then said, 'I'm old enough to be his mother.'

Yale stood very still, and expelled one long noisy gasp of
breath.

'You – you couldn't, Caterina! He's only a boy!'

'He's as adult as you are!'

'He's a boy! You seduced him!'

'Clem, try to see. It was the fraulein originally. She did it to
him – or he started it, I don't know which way it was. But it's a
small island. I came on them one afternoon, both naked, inside
the old fort. I sent her away but somehow the poison spread.
I. . . . After I'd seen him. . . .'

'Oh God, it's incest!'

'You use these stupid old-fashioned terms!'

'You cow! How could you do it with him?' He turned away.
He started walking. She did not stop him. She could not stand
still herself. Swinging about in misery, she burst weeping into
the house and flung herself on to her unmade bed.

For three hours, Yale stood on the north-west edge of the
island, staring paralysed into the sea. In that time, he hardly
moved, except once to unhook his spectacles and wipe his eyes.
His heart laboured and he glared out at the immensity before
him as if challenging it.

She came up quietly behind him, bringing him a glass of
water in which she had dissolved lemon crystals.

He took the glass, thanked her quietly, and drank its contents,
all without looking at her.

'If it makes any difference, Clement, I love and admire you
very much. I'm not fit to be your wife, I know, and I think you
are a saint. Much as I hurt you, your hurt was all for what I
might have done to Philip, wasn't it?'

'Don't be silly! I shouldn't have left you all these months. I
exposed you to temptation.' He looked at her, his face stern.
'I'm sorry for what I said – about incest. You are not related to
Philip, except by marriage. In any case, man is the only creature
that puts a ban on incest. Most other creatures, including the
higher apes, find no harm in it. You can define man as the
species that fears incest. Some psychoanalysts define all mental
illnesses as incest-obsessions, you know. So I'm —'

'Stop!' It was almost a scream. For a moment she fought

with herself, then she said, 'Look, Clem, talk about *us*, for God's sake, not about what the psychoanalysts say or what the higher apes do! Talk about *us*! Think about *us*!'

'I'm sorry, I'm a pedant, I know, but what I meant —'

'And don't, don't, don't apologize to me! I should be apologizing to you, kneeling, begging for forgiveness! Oh, I feel so awful, so guilty, so desperate! You have no idea what I've been through!'

He seized her painfully and held her, looking for the moment very like his son. 'You're getting hysterical! I don't want you kneeling to me, Cat, though thank heavens it has always been one of your dearest traits that you acknowledge your errors in a way I can never manage with mine. You can see what you've done was wrong. I've thought it all over, and I can see the fault was largely mine. I shouldn't have left you isolated here on Kalpeni for so long. This won't make any difference between us, once I've got over the shock. I've thought it over and I think I must write to Philip and tell him that you've told me everything, and that he is not to feel guilty.'

'Clem – how can you – have you no feeling? How can you have forgiven me so easily?'

'I didn't say I'd forgiven you.'

'You just said it!'

'No, I said – Let's not quibble over words. I must forgive you. I have forgiven you.'

She clung to him. 'Then tell me you've forgiven me!'

'I just did.'

'Tell me! Please tell me!'

In a sudden fury, he flung her away from him, crying, 'Damn and blast you, I tell you I have forgiven you, you crazy slut! Why go on?' She fell, sprawling in the sand. Penitently, he stooped to help her up, apologizing for his violence, saying over and over that he had forgiven her. When she was on her feet, they made their way back to the coral-built house, leaving an empty glass lying in the sand. As they went, Caterina said, 'Can you imagine the pain of having to live for a thousand years?'

It was the day after she asked that question that Theodore Devlin arrived on the island.

IV

Almost the entire population of Kalpeni turned out to see the helicopter land on the round chopperport in the centre of the island. Even Vandranasis closed down his little store and followed the thin trickle of spectators northwards.

The great palm leaves clapped together as the machine descended, its WWO insignia gleaming on its black hull. As the blades stopped rotating, Devlin jumped down, followed by his pilot.

Devlin was two or three years Yale's senior, a stocky man in his late forties, well-preserved, and as trim in his appearance as Yale was straggling and untidy. He was a man sharp of face and brain, respected by many, loved by few. Yale, who was wearing nothing but jeans and canvas shoes, strolled over and shook hands with him.

'Fancy seeing you here, Theo! Kalpeni is honoured.'

'Kalpeni is bloody hot! For God's sake, get me in the shade, Clement, before I fry. How you stick it here, I don't know!'

'Gone native, I guess. It's a home from home for me. See my two penguins swimming in the lagoon?'

'Uh.' Devlin was in no mood for small talk. He walked briskly along in a neat light suit, a head shorter than Yale, his muscular movements tight and controlled even over the shifting sand.

At the door of his house, Yale stood aside to let his guest and the pilot, a lanky Indian, enter. Caterina stood inside the room, her face unsmiling. If Devlin was embarrassed at meeting his ex-wife, he gave no sign of it.

'I thought Naples got hot enough. You're living in a damned oven here. How are you, Caterina? You look well. Haven't seen you since you were weeping in the witness box. How does Clement treat you? Not in the style to which you were once accustomed, I hope?'

'You've obviously not come to make yourself pleasant, Theo. Perhaps you and your pilot would care for a drink. Perhaps you were going to introduce him to us?'

After this initial shot across his bows, Devlin pursed his mouth and behaved less pugnaciously. His next remark might even have been construed as an apology. 'Those natives out

133

there annoy me, plastering their fingerprints all over the copter. They haven't taken one elementary step forward since mankind began. They're parasites in every sense of the word! They owe their little all to the fish and the wonderful coconut, both brought to their doorstep by the courtesy of the tides – even their damned island was built for them by countless coral insects!'

'Our culture owes the same sort of debt to other plants and animals, and to the earthworm.'

'At least we pay out debts. However, that's neither here nor there. I just don't share your sentimental attachment to desert islands.'

'We didn't invite you to come here, Theo,' Caterina said. She was still suppressing surprise and anger at seeing him.

Joe appeared and served beer to them all. The pilot stood by the open door to drink his, nervously watching his boss. Devlin, Yale, and Caterina sat down facing each other.

'I gather you got my report?' Yale said. 'That's why you're here, isn't it?'

'You're blackmailing me, Clement. That's why I'm here. What do you want?'

'What?'

'You're blackmailing me. Thomas!' Devlin snapped his fingers as he spoke, and his pilot produced a pistol fitted with what Yale recognized as a silencer; it was the first time he had ever seen one in real life. The pilot stood holding his beer glass in his left hand, sipping casually, but his glance was far from casual. Yale stood up.

'Sit down!' Devlin said, pointing at him. 'Sit down and listen to me, or it will appear later that you had a misunderstanding with a shark while out swimming. You're up against a tough organization, Clement, but you may come to no harm if you behave. What are you after?'

Yale shook his head. 'You're in trouble, Theo, not I. You'd better explain this whole situation.'

'You're always so innocent, aren't you? I'm well aware that that report you sent me, with your assurance that you had let nobody else know the facts, was a thinly camouflaged piece of blackmail. Tell me how I buy your silence.'

Yale looked at his wife; he read in her face the same bafflement he himself felt. Anger with himself grew in him to think that he could not understand Devlin. What was the fellow after? His report had been merely a scientific summary of the cycle by which the Baltic virus had been carried from the Tyrrhenian Sea down to the Antarctic. Dumbly, he shook his head and dropped his eyes to his folded hands. 'I'm sorry, Theo; you know how terribly naïve I am. I just don't get what you are talking about, or why you should think it necessary to point a gun at us.'

'This is more of your paranoia, Theo!' Caterina said. She got up and walked towards Thomas with her hand out. He put the beer down hastily and levelled the pistol at her. 'Give it to me!' she said. He faltered, his gaze evaded hers, she seized the weapon by the barrel, took it from him, and flung it down in one corner of the room.

'Now get out! Go and wait in your helicopter! Take your beer!'

Devlin made a move towards the gun, then stopped. He sat down again, obviously nonplussed. Choosing to ignore Caterina as the only way of salving his dignity, he said, 'Clement, are you serious? You really are such a fool that you don't know what I'm talking about?'

Caterina tapped him on the shoulder. 'You'd better go home. We don't like people to threaten us on this island.'

'Leave him, Cat, let's get out of him whatever extraordinary idea he is nursing. He comes here all the way from Naples, risking his reputation in order to threaten us as if he were a common crook. . . .' Words failed him.

'What do you want, Theo? It's some horrible thing about me, isn't it?'

That restored his humour and some of his confidence. 'No, Caterina, it's not! It's nothing at all to do with you. I lost all interest in you a long long time ago, long before you ran off with this fisherman!' He got up and crossed to the map of the world hanging, dry and fly-spotted, on the wall.

'Clement, you'd better come and look at this. Here's the Baltic. Here's the Med. You tracked the immortality virus all the way from the Baltic right down to the Antarctic. I thought you'd had the wit to grasp how the missing link between Baltic and Mediterranean was forged; I assumed you were suggesting that your silence could be bought on that score. I over-estimated you! You still haven't got it, have you?'

Yale frowned and stroked his face. 'Don't be so superior, Theo. That area was right beyond my bailiwick. I only started in the Tyrrhenian Sea. Of course, if you know what the link is, I'd be tremendously interested.... Presumably it's brought from one sea to the other by a pelagic species. A bird seems a likely agent, but as far as I know nobody has established that the Baltic virus – the immortality virus, you call it – can survive in the body of a bird ... except the Adelie penguin, of course, but there are none of those in the northern hemisphere.'

Taking his arm, Caterina said, 'Darling, he's laughing at you!'

'Ha, Clement, you are a true man of science! Never see what's under your nose because you're sunk up to your eyes in your own pet theories! You gangling fathead! The vital agent was human – *me*! I worked on that virus on a ship in the Baltic, I took it back with me to Naples to WWO HQ, I worked on it in my own private laboratory, I —'

'I don't see how I was supposed to know – Oh! ... Theo, you've found it – you've found a way to infect human beings with the virus!'

The expression on Devlin's face was enough to confirm the truth of that. Yale turned to Caterina. 'Darling, you're right and he's right, I really am a short-sighted idiot! I should have guessed. After all, Naples is situated on the Tyrrhenian Sea – it's just that one never thinks of the term and speaks of it always as the Med.'

'You got there at last!' Devlin said. 'That's how the virus leaked into your Devlin Current. There is a small colony of us in Naples with the virus in our veins. It passes out through the body in inert form, and survives the sewage-processing, so that it is carried out to sea still living – to be digested by the cope-pods, as you managed to discover.'

'The circulation of the blood!'

'What?'

'No matter. A metaphor.'

'Theo – Theo, so you are now ... you have it, do you?'

'Don't be afraid to say it, woman. Yes, I have immortality flowing in my veins.'

Tugging his beard, Yale went and sat down and took a long drink at his beer. He looked from one to the other of them for a long while. At last he said, 'You are something of the true man of science yourself, Theo, aren't you, as well as a career man? You couldn't resist telling us what you know! But leaving that aside, we of course realized that an inoculation of man with the virus was theoretically possible. Cat and I were discussing it until late last night. Do you know what we decided? We decided that even if it were possible to acquire immortality, or shall we say longevity, we should refuse it. We should refuse it because neither of us feels mature enough to bear the responsibility of our emotional and sexual lives for a span of maybe several hundred years.'

'That's pretty negative, isn't it?' Devlin strolled over to the far corner and retrieved the pistol. Before he could slip it into his pocket, Yale stretched out his hand. 'Until you leave, I'll keep it for you. What were you planning to do with it, anyway?'

'I ought to shoot you, Yale.'

'Give it to me! Then you won't be exposed to temptation. You want to keep your little secret, don't you? How long do you think it will be before it becomes public property anyhow? A thing like that can't be kept quiet indefinitely.'

He showed no sign of giving up the gun. He said, 'We've kept our secret for five years. There are fifty of us now, fifty-three, men with power – and some women. Before the secret comes into the open, we are going to be even more powerful: an Establishment. We only need a few years. Meanwhile, we make investments and alliances. Take a look at the way brilliant people have been attracted to Naples these last few years! It's not been just to the WWO or the European Common Government Centre. It's been to my clinic! In another five years, we'll be able to step in and rule Europe – and from there it's just a short step to America and Africa.'

'You see,' Caterina said, 'he is mad, Clem, that sort of sane madness I told you about. But he daren't shoot! He daren't shoot, in case they locked him up for life – and that's a long time for him!'

Recognizing the wild note in his wife's voice, Yale told her to sit down and drink another beer. 'I'm going to take Theo round to see the whales. Come on, Theo! I want to show you what you're up against, with all your fruitless ambitions.'

Theo gave him a sharp look, as if speculating whether he might yield useful information if humoured, evidently concluded that he would, and rose to follow Yale. As he went out, he looked back towards Caterina. She avoided his glance.

It was dazzling to be out in the bright sun again. The crowd was still hanging about the helicopter, chatting intermittently with the pilot, Thomas. Ignoring them, Yale led Devlin past the machine and round the lagoon, blinding in the glare of noon. Devlin gritted his teeth and said nothing. He seemed diminished as they exposed themselves to a landscape almost as bare as an old bone, walking the narrow line between endless blue ocean and the green socket of lagoon.

Without pausing, Yale led on to the north-west strip of beach. It sloped steeply, so that they could see nothing of the rest of the island except the old Portuguese fort, which terminated their view ahead. Grim, black, and ruinous, it might have been some meaningless tumescence erupted by marine forces. As the men tramped towards it, the fort was dwarfed by the intervening carcasses of whales.

Five whales had died here, two of them recently. The giant bodies of the two recently dead still supported rotting flesh, though the skulls gleamed white where the islanders had stripped them for meat and cut out their tongues. The other three had evidently been cast up here at an earlier date, for they were no more than arching skeletons with here and there a fragment of parched skin flapping between rib bones like a curtain in the breeze.

'What have you brought me here for?' Theo was panting, his solid chest heaving.

'To teach you humility and to make you sweat. Look on these works, ye mighty, and despair! These were blue whales, Theo, the largest mammal ever to inhabit this planet! Look at this skeleton! This chap weighed over a hundred tons for sure. He's about eighty feet long.' As he spoke, he stepped into the huge rib cage, which creaked like an old tree as he braced himself momentarily against it. 'A heart beat right here, Theo, that weighed about eight hundredweight.'

'You could have delivered Fifty Amazing Facts of Natural

History, or whatever you call this lecture, in the shade.'

'Ah, but this isn't natural history, Theo. It's highly *un*-natural. These five beasts rotting here once swallowed krill far away in Antarctic waters. They must have gulped down a few mouthfuls of copepod at the same time – copepods that had picked up the Baltic virus. The virus infected the whales. By your admission, that can only have been five years ago, eh? Yet it is long enough to ensure that more blue whales – they were practically extinct from over-fishing, as you know – survived the hazards of immaturity and bred. It would mean too that the breeding period of older specimens was extended. Yet five years is not enough to produce a glut in whales as it is in herrings.'

'What are blue whales doing near the Laccadives in any case?'

'I never found a way to ask them. I only know that these creatures appeared off shore here at full moon, each in a different month. Caterina could tell you – she saw them and told me all about it in her letters. My son Philip was here with her when the last one arrived. Something drove the whales right across the Equator into these seas. Something drove them to cast themselves up on to this beach, raking their stomachs open on the reefs as they did so, to die where you see them lying now. Hang around for ten days, Theo, till the next full moon. You may see another cetaceous suicide.'

There were crabs working in the sand among the barred shadows of the rib cage, burrowing and signalling to each other. When Devlin spoke, anger was back in his voice.

'Okay, you clever trawlerman, tell me the answer to the riddle. It's been revealed to you alone, I suppose, why they kill themselves?'

'They were suffering from side effects, Theo. The side effects of the immortality disease. You know the Baltic virus seems to bring long life – but you haven't had time to find out what else it brings. You've been in so much of a hurry you abandoned scientific method. You didn't want to get any older before you infected yourself. You didn't allow a proper trial period. You may be going to live a thousand years – but *what else is going to happen to you?* What happened to these poor creatures so awful that they could not bear their increase of years? Whatever it was, it was terrible, and soon it will be overtaking you, and

139

all your conspirators sweating it out uneasily in Naples!'

The silencer was extremely effective. The pistol made only a slight hiss, rather like a man blowing a strawberry pip from between his teeth. The bullet made a louder noise as it richocheted off a bleached rib and sped over the ocean. Suddenly Yale was full of movement, moving faster than he had moved in years, lunging forward. He hit Devlin before he fired again. They fell into the sand, Yale on top. He got his foot over Devlin's arm, grasped him with both hands by the windpipe, and bashed his head repeatedly in the sand. When the gun slid loose, he stopped what he was doing, picked up the weapon, and climbed to his feet. Puffing a little, he brushed the sand from his old jeans.

'It wasn't graceful,' he said, glaring down at the purple-faced man rolling at his feet. 'You're a fool!' With a last indignant slap at his legs, he turned and headed back for the coral-built house.

Caterina ran out in terror at the sight of him. The natives surged towards him, thought better of it, and cleared a way for him to pass.

'Clem, Clem, what have you done? You've not shot him?'

'I want a glass of lemonade. It's all right, Cat, my love.... He isn't really hurt.'

When he was sitting down at the table in the cool and drinking the lemonade she mixed him, he began to shake. She had the sense not to say anything until he was ready to speak. She stood beside him, stroking his neck. Presently they saw through the window Devlin coming staggering over the dunes. Without looking in their direction, he made his way over to the helicopter. With Thomas's aid, he climbed in, and in a few moments the engine started and the blades began to turn. The machine lifted, and they watched in silence as it whirled away over the water, eastwards towards the Indian sub-continent. The sound of it died and soon the sight of it was swallowed up in the gigantic sky.

'He was another whale. He came to wreck himself here.'

'You'll have to send a signal to London and tell them everything, won't you?'

'You're right. And tomorrow I must catch some jewfish. I suspect they may be picking up the infection.'

He looked askance at his wife. She had put on her dark glasses while he was gone. Now she took them off again and sat by him, regarding him anxiously.

'I'm not a saint, Cat. Never suggest that again. I'm a bloody liar. I had to tell Theo an awful lie about why the whales ran themselves up our beach.'

'Why?'

'I don't know! Whales have been beaching themselves for years and nobody knows why. Theo would have remembered that if he hadn't been so scared.'

'I meant, why lie to him! You should only lie to people you respect, my mother used to say.'

He laughed. 'Good for her! I lied to scare him. Everyone is going to know about the immortality virus in a few weeks, and I suspect they're all going to want to be infected. I want them all scared. Then perhaps they'll pause, and think what they're asking for – the length of many lifetimes living with their first lifetime's inadequacies.'

'Theo's taking your lie with him. You want that to circulate with the virus?'

He started to clean his spectacles on his handkerchief.

'I do. The world is about to undergo a drastic and radical change. The more slowly that change takes place, the more chance we – all living things, I mean, as well as you and I – have of living quiet and happy as well as lengthy lives. My lie may act as a sort of brake on change. People ought to think what a terrifying thing immortality is – it means sacrificing the mysteries of death. Now how about a bathe, just as if nothing revolutionary had happened?'

As they changed into their swim things, as she stood divested of her clothes, Caterina said, 'I've suddenly had a vision, Clem. Please, I've changed my mind – I want to, I want us both to live as long as we possibly can. I'll sacrifice death for life. You know what I did with Philip? It was only because I suddenly felt my youth slipping from me. Time was against me. I got desperate. With more time ... well, all our values would change, wouldn't they?'

He nodded and said simply, 'You're right, of course.'

They both began to laugh, out of pleasure and excitement. Laughing, they ran down to the lapping ocean, and for a moment it was as if Yale had left all his hesitations behind with his clothes.

As they sat on the edge of the water and snapped their flippers on, he said, 'Sometimes I understand things about people. Theo came here to silence me. But he is an effective man and he was so ineffectual today. It must mean that at bottom he really came to see you, just as you guessed at the time – I reckon he wanted company in all that limitless future he opened up for himself.'

As they sliced out side by side into the warm water, she said without surprise, 'We need time together, Clem, time to understand each other.'

They dived together, down in a trail of bubbles below the sparkling surface, startling the fish. Flipping over on his side, Yale made for the channel that led out to the open sea. She followed, glad in her heart, as she was destined to do and be for the next score and a half of centuries.

Under the weight of sunlight, the low hills abased themselves. To the three people sitting behind the driver of the hover, it seemed that pools of liquid – something between oil and water – formed constantly on the pitted road ahead, to disappear miraculously as they reached the spot. In all the landscape, this optical illusion was the only hint that moisture existed.

The passengers had not spoken for some while. Now the Pakistani Health Official, Firoz Ayub Khan, turned to his guests and said, 'Within an hour, we shall be into Calcutta. Let us hope and pray that the air-conditioning of this miserable machine holds out so long!'

The woman by his side gave no sign that she heard him, continuing to stare forward through her dark glasses; she left it to her husband to make an appropriate response. She was a slender woman of dark complexion, her narrow face made notable by its generous mouth. Her black hair, gathered over one shoulder, was disordered from the four-hour drive down from the hill station.

Her husband was a tall spare man, apparently in his mid-forties, who wore old-fashioned steel-rimmed spectacles. His face in repose carried an eroded look, as if he had spent many years gazing at just such countries as the one outside. He said, 'It was good of you to consent to letting us use this slow mode of transport, Dr. Khan. I appreciate your impatience to get back to work.'

'Well, well, I am impatient, that is perfectly true. Calcutta needs me – and you too, now you are recovered from your illness. And Mrs. Yale also, naturally.' It was difficult to determine whether Khan's voice concealed sarcasm.

'It is well worth seeing the land at first hand, in order to appreciate the magnitude of the problems against which Pakistan and India are battling.'

Clement Yale had noted before that his speeches intended to mollify the health official seemed to produce the opposite effect. Khan said, 'Mr. Yale, what problems do you refer to? There is no problem anywhere, only the old satanic problem of the human condition, that is all.'

'I was referring to the evacuation of Calcutta and its attendant difficulties. You would admit they constituted a problem, surely?'

This sort of verbal jostling had broken out during the last half-hour of the ride.

'Well, well, naturally where you have a city containing some twenty-five million people, there you expect to find a few problems, wouldn't you agree, Mrs. Yale? Rather satanic problems, maybe – but always stemming from and rooted in the human condition. That is why executives such as ourselves are always needed, isn't it?'

Yale gestured beyond the window, where broken carts lay by the roadside. 'This is the first occasion in modern times that a city has simply bogged itself down and had to be abandoned. I would call that a special problem.'

He hardly listened to Khan's long and complicated answer; the health official was always involving himself in contradictions from which verbiage could not rescue him. He stared instead out of the window as the irreparable world of heat slid past. The carts and cars had been fringing the road for some while – indeed, almost all the way from the hospital in the hills, where East Madras was still green. Here, nearer Calcutta, their skeletal remains lay thicker. Between the shafts of some of the carts lay bones, many of them no longer recognizable as those of bullocks; lesser skeletons toothed the wilderness beyond the road.

The hover-driver muttered constantly to himself. The dead formed no obstacle to their progress; the living and half-living had yet to be considered. Pouring out of the great ant-heap ahead were knots of human beings, solitary figures, family groups, men, women, children, the more fortunate with beasts of burden or handcarts or bicycles to support themselves or their scanty belongings. Blindly they moved forward, going they hardly knew whither, treading over those who had fallen, not raising their heads to avoid the oncoming hover-ambulance.

For centuries, the likes of these people had been pouring into Calcutta from the dying hinterland. Nine months ago, when the government of the city had fallen and the Indian Congress had announced that the city would be abandoned, the stream had

144

reversed its direction. The refugees became refugees again.

Caterina behind her dark glasses took in the parched images. Mankind driven always drive the bare foot on the way the eternal road of earth and no real destination only the way to water and longer grass. Will we be able to get a drink there always the stone beneath the passing instep.

She said, 'I suppose one shouldn't hope for a shower when we get there.'

Ayub Khan said, 'The air-condition is not all it should be, lady. Hence the sensation of heat. There has not been proper servicing of the vehicle. I shall make some appropriate complaints when we arrive, never wonder!'

Jerking to avoid a knot of refugees, the hover rounded a shoulder of hill. The endless deltaic plain of the Ganges stretched before them, fading in the far distance, annihilating itself in its own vision of sun.

To one side of the track stood a grim building, the colour of mud, its walls rising silent and stark. Not a fortress, not a temple: the meaningless functionalism, now functionless, of some kind of factory. Beside it, one or two goats scampered and vanished.

Ayub Khan uttered a command to the driver. The hover slid to one side. The road near at hand was temporarily deserted. Their machine bumped over the ditch and drifted towards the factory, raising dust high as it went. Its engines died, it sank to the ground. Ayub Khan was reaching behind him for the holstered rifle on the rack above their heads.

'What's this place?' Yale asked, rousing himself.

'A temporary diversion, Mr. Yale, that will not occupy us for more than the very moment. Maybe you and your lady will care to climb out with me for a moment and exercise? Go steadily remembering you were ill.'

'I have no wish to climb out, Dr. Khan. We are urgently needed in Calcutta. What are we stopping for? What is this place?'

The Pakistani doctor smiled and took down a box of cartridges. As he loaded the rifle, he said, 'I forget you are not only recently sick but also immortal and must take the greatest care. But the desperate straits of Calcutta will wait for us for ten minutes' break, I assure you. Recall, the human condition goes on for ever.'

The human condition goes on for ever sticks stones bows and arrows shotguns nuclear weapons quescharges and the foot and face going down into the dust the perfect place for death. She stirred and said, 'The human condition goes on for ever, Dr. Khan, but we are expected in Dalhousie Square today.'

As he opened the door, he smiled. 'Expectancy is a pleasing part of our life, Mrs. Yale.'

The Yales looked at each other. The driver was climbing down after Ayub Khan, and gesticulating excitedly. 'His relish of power likewise,' Yale said.

'We cadged the ride.'

'The ride – not the moralizing! Still, part of abrasion.'

'Feeling right, Clem?'

'Perfectly.' To show her, he climbed out of the vehicle with a display of energy. He was still angry with himself for contracting cholera in the middle of a job where every man's capacity was stretched to the utmost; the dying metropolis was a stewpot of disease.

As he helped Cat down, they felt the heat of the plains upon them. It was the heat of a box, allowing no perspective but its own. The moisture in it stifled their lungs; with each breath, they felt their shoulders prickle and their bodies weep.

Ayub Khan was striding forward, rifle ready for action, the driver chattering excitedly by him, carrying spare ammunition.

Time, suffering from a slow wound, was little past midday, so that the derelict factory was barren of shadow. Nevertheless, the two English moved instinctively towards it, following the Pakistanis, feeling as they went old heat rebuffed from the walls of the great fossil.

'Old cement factory.'

'Cementary.'

'Mortarl remaniés. . . .'

'Yes, here's an acre stone indeed. . . .'

The rifle went off loudly.

'Missed!' said Ayub Khan cheerfully, rubbing the top of his head with his free hand. He ran forward, the driver close behind him. Ramshackle remains of a metal outbuilding stood to one side of the factory façade; a powdered beam of it collapsed as the men trotted past and disappeared from view.

And the termites too have their own empires and occasions and never over-extend their capacities they create and destroy on a major time-scale yet they have no aspirations. Man became sick when he discovered he lived on a planet when his world became finite his aspirations grew infinite and what the hell could those idiots be doing?

Switching on his pocket fan, Yale walked up the gritty steps of the factory. The double wooden door, once barred, had long since been broken down. He paused on the threshold and looked back at his wife, standing indecisively in the heat.

'Coming in?'

She made an impatient gesture and followed. He watched her. He had watched that walk for almost four centuries now, still without tiring of it. It was *her* walk: independent, yet not entirely; selfconscious, yet, in a true sense, self-forgetting; a stride that did not hurry, that was neither old nor young; a woman's walk; Cat's walk; a cat-walk. It defined her as clearly as her voice. He realized that in the preoccupations of the last two months, in doomed Calcutta and in the hospital ward, he had often forgotten her, the living her.

As she came up the steps level with him, he took her arm.

'Feelings?'

'Specifically, irritation with Khan foremost. Secondarily, knowledge we need our Khans. . . .'

'Yes, but how now to you?'

'Our centuries – as ever. Limit gravely areas of non-predictability in human relations among Caucasian-Christian community. Consequent accumulation of staleness abraded by unknown factors.'

'Such as Khan?'

'Sure. You similarly abraded, Clem?'

'He has chafage value. Ditto all sub-continent.'

His fingers released her arm. The brown flesh ever young left no sign of the ephemeral touch. But the Baltic virus would have quickly healed the harshest grip he could have bestowed.

They looked into the old chaos of the factory, moved in over rubble. A corpse lay in a side office, open-mouthed, hollow, without stink; something slid away from under, afraid for its own death.

From the passage beyond, noise, echoey and conflicting.

'Back to the float?'

'This old temple to India's failure —' He stopped. Two small goats, black of face and beardless, came at a smart clip from the back of the darkness ahead, eyes – in Ayub Khan't pet word – 'satanic', came forward swerving and bleating.

And from the far confusion of shadow, Ayub Khan stopped and raised his rifle. Yale lifted a hand as the shot came.

Temples and the conflicting desires to make and destroy ascetic priests and fat ones my loving husband still had his tender core unspoilt for more years.

The goats tumbling past them, Yale sagging to the ground, the noise of the shot with enormous power to extend itself far into the future, Cat transfixed, and somewhere a new ray of light searching down as if part of the roof had given way.

Rushing forward, Ayub Khan gave Cat back her ability to move; she turned to Yale, who was already getting to his feet again. The Pakistani calling, his driver behind him.

'My dear and foolish Mr. Yale! Have I not rifled you, I sincerely trust! What terrible disaster if you are dead! How did I know you crept secretly into this place? My godfathers! How you did scare me! Driver! *Pani lao, jhaldi!*'

He fussed anxiously about Yale until the driver returned from the ambulance with a beaker of water. Yale drank it and said, 'Thank you, I'm perfectly well, Dr. Khan, and you missed me, fortunately.'

'What do you imagine you were doing?' Cat asked.

Hold your hands together so they will not shake and your thighs if he had been killed murder most dreaded of crimes even to short-livers and this idiot —

'Madam, you must surely see that I was shooting at the two goats. Though I hope thoroughly that I am a good Muslim, I was shooting at those two damned satanic goats. That action needs not any justification, surely?'

She was still shaking and trying to recover her poise. High abrasion value okay! 'Goats? In here?'

'Mrs. Yale, the driver, and I have seen these goats from the road and chase after them. Because the back of this factory is broken, they escape from us into here. We follow. Little do we know that you creep secretly in from the front! What a scare! My godfathers!'

As he paused to light a mescahale, she saw his hand was shaking; the observation restored a measure of sympathy for the man. She further relaxed her pulse-count by a side-glance at Yale, for their glances by now, cryptic as their personal conversations, told them as much; certain the shot was careless, he was already more interested in the comedy of Ayub Khan's reactions than his own.

Yes many would find him a negative man not seeing that the truth is he has the ability to add to his own depths other people's. He stands there while others talk saintly later he will deliver the nub of the matter. My faith of which he would disapprove indeed I have an obligation not to be all faith must also fill my abrasion quota for him!

'You know, I really hate these little satanic goats! In Pakistan and India they cause the chief damage to territory and the land will never revive while goats are upon it. In my own province, I watch them climb the trees to eat up new tender shoots. So the latest laws to execute goats, reinforced with rewards of two new-rupees per hoof, are so much to my thinking, more than you Europeans can understand. . . .'

'That is certainly true, Dr. Khan,' Yale said. 'I fully share your dislike of the destructive power of the goat. Unfortunately, such animals are a part and parcel of our somewhat patchy history. The hogs that ensured that the early forests, once felled by stone axes, did not grow again, and the sheep and goats that formed man's traditional food supplies, have left as indelible a mark on Europe as on Asia and elsewhere. The eroded shores of the Mediterranean and the barren lands all round that sea are their doing, in league with man.'

Does the pressure of my thought make him speak of early mankind now? Through these centuries glad and stern I have come to see man's progress as a blind attempt to escape from those hopeful buffoons so exposed to chance yet chance beats down like weather whatever you cover your back with we know who live a long while that the heart stagnates without abrasion and the great abrader is chance.

Now Ayub Khan had perked up and was smiling over the fumes of his mescahale, gesturing with one hand.

'Now, now, don't be bitter, Mr. Yale – nobody denies that the Europeans have their share of minor troubles! But let's admit while we are being really frank that they also have all the luck, don't they? I mean to say, to give one example, the Baltic virus happened in their part of the world, didn't it?, just like the Industrial Revolution many hundreds of years ago.'

'Your part of the world, Doctor, has enough to contend with without longevity as well!'

'Precisely so! What is an advantage to you Europeans, and to the Americans behind their long disgraceful isolationism, is a disadvantage entirely to the unlucky Asiatic nations, that is what I am saying. That is precisely why our governments have made longevity illegal – as you well know, a Pakistani suffers capital punishment if he is found to be a long-liver, just because we do not solve our satanic population problem so very easily as Europe. So we are condemned to our life-expectancy of merely forty-seven years average, against your thousands! How can that be fair, Mr. Yale? We are all human beings, wherever we live on the planet of Earth, Equator or Pole, my godfathers!'

Yale shrugged. 'I don't pretend to call it fair. Nobody calls it fair. It just happens that "fairness" is not a built-in natural law. Man invented the concept of justice – it's one of his better ideas – but the rest of the universe, unfortunately, doesn't give a damn for it.'

'It's very easy for you to be smug.'

He looks so angry and hurt his skin almost purple his eyeballs yellow rather like a goat himself not a good representative of his race. But the antipathy can never be overcome the haves and the have-nots the Neanderthal and the Cro-Magnon the rich and the poor we can never give what we have. We should get back into the float and drive on. I'd like to wash my hair. The goats moved endlessly across the plain with every step they took the great enchanted ruin behind them crumbled into a material like straw and as they went and multiplied long grasses sprang out of the human corpses littering the plain and the goats capered forward and ate.

'Smugness does not enter the matter. There are the facts and —'

'Facts! Facts! Oh, your satanic British factualism! I suppose you call the many goats facts? How does it come about, ask yourself, how does it come about that these goats can live forever and I cannot, for all my superior reasoning powers?'

Yale said, 'I fear I can only answer you with more factualism. We know now, as for many years we did not, that the Baltic virus is extraterrestrial in origin, most probably arriving on this planet by tektite. To exist in a living organism, the virus needs a certain rare dynamic condition in the mitochondria of cells known as rubmission – the Red Vibrations of the popular press – and this it finds in only a handful of terrestrial types, among which are such disparate creatures as copepods, Adelie penguins, herring, man, and goats and sheep.'

'We have enough trouble with this satanic drought without immortal goats!'

'Immortality – as you call longevity – is not proof against famine. Although the goats' reproductive period is in theory infinitely extended, they are still dying for lack of nourishment.'

'Not so fast as the humans!'

'Vigilance will certainly be needed when the rains come.'

'You immortals can afford to wait that long!'

'We are *long-livers*, Dr. Khan.'

'My godfathers, define for me the difference between longevity and immortality in a way that makes sense to a short-lived Pakistan man!'

'Immortality can afford to forget death and, in consequence, the obligations of life. Longevity can't.'

'Let's get on to Calcutta,' Cat said. Vultures perched on the top of the stained façade: she found herself vulnerable to their presence. She walked across to the doorway. The driver had already slipped out at the back of the factory.

On the long road the humble figures. When did that woman last have a bath to have to bear children in such conditions. This is what life is all about this is why we left the stainless towers of our cooler countries their comforts and compromises in the broken down parts of the world there is no pretence about what life is really like Clem and I and the other long-livers are merely clever western artefacts of suspended decay everyday we know that one day we shall have to tumble into slag each our own Calcutta oh for God's sake satanically can it!

The men were following her. She saw now that Ayub Khan had laid a hand on Yale's arm and was talking in more friendly fashion.

The hover's door had been left open. It would be abominably

hot in there.

Two skeletal goats cross the road, ears lop, parading before two refugees. The refugees were men walking barefoot with sticks, bags of belongings slung on their backs. For them, the goats would represent not only food but the reward the government offered for hooves. Breaking from their trance, they waved their arms and wielded their sticks. One of the goats was struck across its serrated backbone. It broke into a trot. Ayub Khan raised his rifle and fired at the other goat from almost point-blank range.

He hit it in the stomach. The creature's back legs collapsed. Piddling blood, it attempted to drag itself off the road, away from Ayub Khan. The two refugees fell on it, jostling each other with scarecrow gestures. With an angry shout, Ayub Khan ran forward and prodded them out of the way with the rifle barrel. He called to the driver, who came at a trot, pulling out a knife; squatting, he chopped at the goat's legs repeatedly until the hooves were severed; by that time, the animal appeared to be dead.

The government will pay. Like all Indian legislation this bounty favours the rich and the strong at the expense of the poor and weak. Like everything else cool Delhi justice melts in the heat.

Above the factory entrance, the vultures shuffled and nodded in understanding.

Straightening, Ayub Khan gestured to the two refugees, inviting them to drag the body off. They stood stupidly, not coming forward, perhaps fearing attack. Clapping his hands once, Ayub Khan dismissed them and turned away, circling the goat's carcass.

To Caterina he said, 'Just allow me one further moment, madam, while I shoot down this second goat. It is my public duty.'

To sit in the shade of the ambulance or go and watch him carry out his public duty. No choice really he shall not think us squeamish we don't need his uncouth exhibition to tell us that even we are in the general league with death. Remember after Clem and I returned from the bullfight in Seville Philip no more than seven years old I suppose asked Who won? and cried when we laughed. We must be brave bulls *toros bravos* who live on something less prone to eclipse than hope.

Yale said, 'Follow and these can at least claim what's left.'

'Sure, and we attend caprine execution.'

'Gory caprice!'

'Goat kaputt.'

'You over-hot?'

'Just delay. Thanks.' Smiles in the general blindness.

'Delay produce of no goal within fulfilment.'

'Vice versa too, suppose.'

'Suppose. Eastern thing. Hence Industrial Rev never took here.'

'Factory example, Clem.'

'So, quite. Wrongly situated regards supply, power, consumers, distribution.'

Calcutta itself a similar example on enormous satanic scale. Situated on Hooghli, river now almost entirely silted up despite dramatic attempts. And the centuries-old division between India and Pakistan like a severed limb the refugees breaking down all attempts at organization finally the water-table under the city hopelessly poisoned by sewage mass eruptions of disease scampering mesolithic men crouching in their cave exchanging illnesses viruses use mankind as walking cities.

'Calcutta somewhat ditto.'

'Ssh, founded by East India merchant, annoy Khan!'

They looked at each other, just perceptibly grinning, as they walked round to the back of the factory.

The surviving goat was white-bodied, marked with brown specks; its head and face were dark brown or black, its eyes yellow. It walked under a series of low *bashas*, now deserted, apparently once used as huts for the factory-owners. Their thatched walls, ruinous, gave them an air of transparency. The light speared them. Beyond them, the undistinguished lump of Calcutta lay amid the nebulous areas where land met sky.

Ravenously, the goat reached up and dragged at the palm leaves covering a *basha* roof. As a section of the roof came down in a cascade of dust, Ayub Khan fired. Kicking up its bounty-laden heels, the goat disappeared among the huts.

Ayub Khan reloaded. 'Generally, I am a satanically sound marksman. It is this confounded heat putting me off that I chiefly complain of. Why don't you have a shot, Yale, and see if you do a lot better? You English are such sportsmen!' He offered the rifle.

'No, thanks, Doctor. I'm rather anxious for us to be getting on to Calcutta.'

'Calcutta is just a tragedy – let it wait, let it wait! The hunting blood is up! First, let's have a little fun with this terrible satanic goat!'

'Fun? It was public duty a moment ago!'

Ayub Khan looked at him. 'What are you doing here, anyway, with your pretty wife? Isn't this all *fun* for you as well as public duty? Did you have to come to our satanic Asia, ask yourself?'

Isn't he right don't we eternally have to redeem ourselves for the privilege of living and seeing other life by sacrificing death Clement must have said the same thing often to himself by sacrificing death did we not also sacrifice the norms of normal life in this long-protracted life is not our atonement our fun helping supervise the evacuation of Calcutta our goat-shoot. In his eyes we can never redeem ourselves only in our own eyes.

'Instead of papering over the cracks at home, Doctor, we prefer to stand on the brink of your chasms. You must forgive us. Go and shoot your goat and then we will proceed to Calcutta.'

'It is very very curious that when you seem to be talking better sense, I am not able to understand you. Driver, *idhar ao*!'

Gesturing to the driver, the health official disappeared behind the threadbare huts.

On the road, the refugees still trod, losing themselves in the mists of distance and time. Individuality was forgotten: there were only organisms, moving according to certain laws, performing antique motions. In the Hooghli, water flowed, bringing down silt from source to delta, the dredgers rusting, the arteries clogging, little speckled crabs waving across grey sandbanks.

The Worm That Flies

The traveller was too absorbed in his reveries to notice when the snow began to fall. He walked slowly, his stiff and elaborate garments, fold over fold, ornament over ornament, standing out from his body like a wizard's tent.

The road along which he travelled had been falling into a great valley, and was increasingly hemmed in by walls of mountain. On several occasions, it had seemed that a way out of these huge accumulations of earth matter could not be found, that the geological puzzle was insoluble, the chthonian arrangement of discord irresolvable: and then vale and drumlin created between them a new direction, a surprise, an escape, and the way took fresh heart and plunged recklessly still deeper into the encompassing upheaval.

The traveller, whose name to his wife was Tapmar and to the rest of the world Argustal, followed this natural harmony in complete paraesthesia, so close was he in spirit to the atmosphere prevailing here. So strong was this bond, that the freak snowfall merely heightened his rapport.

Though the hour was only midday, the sky became the intense blue-grey of dusk. The Forces were nesting in the sun again, obscuring its light. Consequently, Argustal was scarcely able to detect when the layered and fractured bulwark of rock on his left side, the top of which stood unseen perhaps a mile above his head, became patched by artificial means, and he entered the domain of the human company of Or.

As the way made another turn, he saw a wayfarer before him, heading in his direction. It was a great pine, immobile until warmth entered the world again and sap stirred enough in its wooden sinews for it to progress slowly forward once more. He brushed by its green skirts, apologetic but not speaking.

This encounter was sufficient to raise his consciousness above its trance level. His extended mind, which had reached out to embrace the splendid terrestrial discord hereabouts, now shrank to concentrate again on the particularities of his situation, and he saw that he had arrived at Or.

The way bisected itself, unable to choose between two equally unpromising ravines, and Argustal saw a group of humans standing statuesque in the left-hand fork. He went towards them, and stood there silent until they should recognize his presence. Behind him, the wet snow crept into his footprints.

These humans were well advanced into the New Form, even as Argustal had been warned they would be. There were five of them standing here, their great brachial extensions bearing some tender brownish foliage, and one of them attenuated to a height of almost twenty feet. The snow lodged in their branches and in their hair.

Argustal waited for a long span of time, until he judged the afternoon to be well advanced, before growing impatient. Putting his hands to his mouth, he shouted fiercely at them, 'Ho then, Treemen of Or, wake you from your arboreal sleep and converse with me. My name is Argustal to the world, and I travel to my home in far Talembil, where the seas run pink with the spring plankton. I need from you a component for my para-patterner, so rustle yourselves and speak, I beg!'

Now the snow had gone, and a scorching rain driven away its traces. The sun shone again, but its disfigured eye never looked down into the bottom of this ravine. One of the humans shook a branch, scattering water drops all round, and made preparation for speech.

This was a small human, no more than ten feet high, and the old primate form which it had begun to abandon perhaps a couple of million years ago was still in evidence. Among the gnarls and whorls of its naked flesh, its mouth was discernible; this it opened and said, 'We speak to you, Argustal-to-the-world. You are the first ape-human to fare this way in a great time. Thus you are welcome, although you interrupt our search for new ideas.'

'Have you found any new ideas?' Argustal asked, with his customary boldness.

'Indeed. But it is better for our senior to tell you of it, if he so judges good.'

It was by no means clear to Argustal whether he wished to hear what the new idea was, for the Tree-men were known for their deviations into incomprehensibility. But there was a minor furore among the five, as if private winds stirred in their branches, and he settled himself on a boulder, preparing to wait.

His own quest was so important that all impediments to its fulfilment seemed negligible.

Hunger overtook him before the senior spoke. He hunted about and caught slow-galloping grubs under logs, and snatched a brace of tiny fish from the stream, and a handful of nuts from a bush that grew by the stream.

Night fell before the senior spoke. Tall and knotty, his vocal chords were clamped within his gnarled body, and he spoke by curving his branches until his finest twigs, set against his mouth, could be blown through, to give a slender and whispering version of language. The gesture made him seem curiously like a maiden who spoke with her finger cautiously to her lips.

'Indeed we have a new idea, O Argustal-to-the-world, though it may be beyond your grasping or our expressing. We have perceived that there is a dimension called time, and from this we have drawn a deduction.

'We will explain dimensional time simply to you like this. We know that all things have lived so long on Earth that their origins are forgotten. What we can remember carries from that lost-in-the-mist thing up to this present moment; it is the time we inhabit, and we are used to think of it as all the time there is. But we men of Or have reasoned that this is not so.'

'There must be other past times in the lost distances of time,' said Argustal, 'but they are nothing to us because we cannot touch them as we can our own pasts.'

As if this remark had never been, the silvery whisper continued, 'As one mountain looks small when viewed from another, so the things in our past that we remember look small from the present. But suppose we moved back to that past to look at this present! We could not see it – yet we know it exists. And from this we reason that there is still more time in the future, although we cannot see it.'

For a long while, the night was allowed to exist in silence, and then Argustal said, 'Well, I don't see that as being very wonderful reasoning. We know that, if the Forces permit, the sun will shine again tomorrow, don't we?'

The small tree-man who had first spoken, said, 'But "tomorrow" is expressional time. *We* have discovered that tomorrow exists in dimensional time also. It is real already, as real as yesterday.'

'Holy spirits!' thought Argustal to himself, 'why did I get involved in philosophy?' Aloud he said, 'Tell me of the deduction you have drawn from this.'

Again the silence, until the senior drew together his branches and whispered from a bower of twiggy fingers, 'We have proved that tomorrow is no surprise. It is as unaltered as today or yesterday, merely another yard of the path of time. But we comprehend that things change, don't we? You comprehend that, don't you?'

'Of course. You yourselves are changing, are you not?'

'It is as you say, although we no longer recall what we were before, for that thing is become too small back in time. So: if time is all of the same quality, then it has no change, and thus cannot force change. So: there is another unknown element in the world that forces change!'

Thus in their fragmentary whispers they reintroduced sin into the world.

Because of the darkness, a need for sleep was induced in Argustal. With the senior tree-man's permission, he climbed up into his branches and remained fast asleep until dawn returned to the fragment of sky above the mountains and filtered down to their retreat. Argustal swung to the ground, removed his outer garments, and performed his customary exercises. Then he spoke to the five beings again, telling them of his parapatterner, and asking for certain stones.

Although it was doubtful whether they understood what he was doing, they gave him permission, and he moved round about the area, searching for a necessary stone, his senses blowing into nooks and crannies for it like a breeze.

The ravine was blocked at its far end by a rock fall, but the stream managed to pour through the interstices of the detritus into a yet lower defile. Climbing painfully, Argustal scrambled over the mass of broken rock to find himself in a cold and moist passage, a mere cavity between two great thighs of mountain. Here the light was dim, and the sky could hardly be seen, so far did the rocks overhang on the many shelves of strata overhead. But Argustal scarcely looked up. He followed the stream where it flowed into the rock itself, to vanish forever from human view.

He had been so long at his business, trained himself over so many millennia, that the stones almost spoke to him, and he became more certain than ever that he would find a stone to fit in with his grand design.

It was there. It lay just above the water, the upper part of it polished. When he had prised it out from the surrounding pebbles and gravel, he lifted it and could see that underneath it was slightly jagged, as if a smooth gum grew black teeth. He was surprised, but as he squatted to examine it, he began to see what was necessary to the design of his parapatterner was precisely some such roughness. At once, the next step of the design revealed itself, and he saw for the first time the whole thing as it would be in its entirety. The vision disturbed and excited him.

He sat where he was, his blunt fingers round the rough-smooth stone, and for some reason he began to think about his wife Pamitar. Warm feelings of love ran through him, so that he smiled to himself and twitched his brows.

By the time he stood up and climbed out of the defile, he knew much about the new stone. His nose-for-stones sniffed it back to times when it was much larger affair, when it occupied a grand position on a mountain, when it was engulfed in the bowels of the mountain, when it had been cast up and shattered down, when it had been a component of a bed of rock, when that rock had been ooze, when it had been a gentle rain of volcanic sediment, showering through an unbreathable atmosphere and filtering down through warm seas in an early and unknown place.

With tender respect, he tucked the stone away in a large pocket and scrambled back along the way he had come. He made no farewell to the five of Or. They stood mute together, branch-limbs interlocked, dreaming of the dark sin of change.

Now he made haste for home, travelling first through the borderlands of Old Crotheria and then through the region of Tamia, where there was only mud. Legends had it that Tamia had once known fertility, and that speckled fish had swam in streams between forests; but now mud conquered everything, and the few villages were of baked mud, while the roads were dried mud, the sky was the colour of mud, and the few mud-coloured humans who chose for their own mud-stained reasons to live here had scarcely any antlers growing from their shoulders and seemed about to deliquesce into mud. There wasn't a decent stone anywhere about the place. Argustal met a tree called David-by-the-moat-that-dries which was moving into his own home region. Depressed by the everlasting brown-ness of Tamia, he begged a ride from it, and climbed into its branches. It was old and gnarled, its branches and roots equally hunched, and it spoke in grating syllables of its few ambitions.

As he listened, taking pains to recall each syllable while he waited long for the next, Argustal saw that David spoke by much the same means as the people of Or had done, stuffing whistling twigs to an orifice in its trunk; but whereas it seemed that the tree-men were losing the use of their vocal chords, it seemed that the man-tree was developing some from the stringy integuments of its fibres, so that it became a nice problem as to which was inspired by which, which copied which, or whether – for both sides seemed so self-absorbed that this also was a possibility – they had come on a mirror-image of perversity independently.

'Motion is the prime beauty,' said David-by-the-moat-that-dries, and took many degrees of the sun across the muddy sky to say it. 'Motion is in me. There is no motion in the ground. In the ground there is not motion. All that the ground contains is without motion. The ground lies in quiet and to lie in the ground is not to be. Beauty is not in the ground. Beyond the ground is the air. Air and ground make all there is and I would be of the ground and air. I was of the ground and of the air but I will be of the air alone. If there is ground, there is another ground. The leaves fly in the air and my longing goes with them but they are only part of me because I am of wood. O, Argustal, you know not the pains of wood!'

Argustal did not indeed, for long before this gnarled speech was spent, the moon had risen and the silent muddy night had fallen, and he was curled asleep in David's distorted branches, the stone in his deep pockets.

Twice more he slept, twice more watched their painful progress along the unswept tracks, twice more joined converse with the melancholy tree – and when he woke again, all the heavens were stacked with fleecy cloud that showed blue between, and low hills lay ahead. He jumped down. Grass grew here. Pebbles littered the track. He howled and shouted with pleasure.

Crying his thanks he set off across the heath.

'. . . growth . . .' said David-by-the-moat-that-dries.

The heath collapsed and gave way to sand, fringed by sharp grass that scythed at Argustal's skirts as he went by. He ploughed across the sand. This was his own country, and he rejoiced, taking his bearing from the occasional cairn that pointed a finger of shade across the sand. Once, one of the Forces flew over, so that for a moment of terror the world was plunged in night, thunder growled, and a paltry hundred drops of rain spattered down; then it was already on the far confines of the sun's domain, plunging away – no matter where!

Few animals, fewer birds, still survived. In the sweet deserts of Outer Talembil, they were especially rare. Yet Argustal passed a bird sitting on a cairn, its hooded eye bleared with a million years of danger. It fluttered one wing at sight of him, in tribute to old reflexes, but he respected the hunger in his belly too much to try to dine on sinews and feathers, and the bird appeared to recognize the fact.

He was nearing home. The memory of Pamitar was sharp before him, so that he could follow it like a scent. He passed another of his kind, an old ape wearing a red mask hanging almost to the ground; they barely gave each other a nod of recognition. Soon on the idle skyline he saw the blocks that marked Gornilo, the first town of Talembil.

The ulcerated sun travelled across the sky. Stoically, Argustal travelled across the intervening dunes, and arrived in the shadow of the white blocks of Gornilo.

No one could recollect now – recollection was one of the lost things that many felt privileged to lose – what factors had determined certain features of Gornilo's architecture. This was an ape-human town, and perhaps in order to construct a memorial to yet more distant and dreadful things, the first inhabitants of the town had made slaves of themselves and of the other creatures that now were no more, and erected these great cubes that now showed signs of weathering, as if they tired at last of swinging their shadows every day about their bases. The ape-humans who lived here were the same ape-humans who had always lived here; they sat as untiringly under their mighty memorial blocks as they had always done – calling now to Argustal as he passed as languidly as one flicks stones across the surface of a lake – but they could recollect no longer if or how they had shifted the blocks across the desert; it might be that that forgetfulness formed an integral part of being as permanent as the granite of the blocks.

Beyond the blocks stood the town. Some of the trees here were visitors, bent on becoming as David-by-the-moat-that-dries was, but most grew in the old way, content with ground and indifferent to motion. They knotted their branches this way and slatted their twigs that way, and humped their trunks the other way, and thus schemed up ingenious and ever-changing homes for the tree-going inhabitants of Gornilo.

At last Argustal came to his home, on the far side of the town.

The name of his home was Cormok. He pawed and patted and licked it first before running lightly up its trunk to the living-room.

Pamitar was not there.

He was not surprised at this, hardly even disappointed, so serene was his mood. He walked slowly about the room, sometimes swinging up to the ceiling in order to view it better, licking and sniffing as he went, chasing the after-images of his wife's presence. Finally, he laughed and fell into the middle of the floor.

'Settle down, boy!' he said.

Sitting where he had dropped, he unloaded his pockets, taking out the five stones he had acquired in his travels and laying them aside from his other possessions. Still sitting, he disrobed, enjoying doing it inefficiently. Then he climbed into the sand bath.

While Argustal lay there, a great howling wind sprang up, and in a moment the room was plunged into sickly greyness. A prayer went up outside, a prayer flung by the people at the unheeding Forces not to destroy the sun. His lower lip moved in a gesture at once of content and contempt; he had forgotten the prayers of Talembil. This was a religious city. Many of the Unclassified congregated here from the waste miles, people or animals whose minds had dragged them aslant from what they were into rococo forms that more exactly defined their inherent qualities, until they resembled forgotten or extinct forms, or forms that had no being till now, and acknowledged no common cause with any other living thing – except in this desire to preserve the festering sunlight from further ruin.

Under the fragrant grains of the bath, submerged all but for head and a knee and hand, Argustal opened wide his perceptions to all that might come: and finally thought only what he had often thought while lying there – for the armouries of cerebration had long since been emptied of all new ammunition, whatever the tree-men of Or might claim – that in such baths, under such an unpredictable wind, the major life forms of Earth, men and trees, had probably first come at their impetus to change. But change itself ... had there been a much older thing blowing about the world that everyone had forgotten?

For some reason, that question aroused discomfort in him. He felt dimly that there was another side of life than content and happiness; all beings felt content and happiness; but were those qualities a unity, or were they not perhaps one side only of a – of a shield?

He growled. Start thinking gibberish like that and you ended up human with antlers on your shoulders!

Brushing off the sand, he climbed from the bath, moving more swiftly than he had done in countless time, sliding out of his home, down to the ground without bothering to put on his clothes.

He knew where to find Pamitar. She would be beyond the town, guarding the parapatterner from the tattered angry beggars of Talembil.

The cold wind blew, with an occasional slushy thing in it that made a being blink and wonder about going on. As he strode through the green and swishing heart of Gornilo, treading among the howlers who knelt casually everywhere in rude prayer, Argustal looked up at the sun. It was visible by fragments, torn through tree and cloud. Its face was blotched and pimpled, sometimes obscured altogether for an instant at a time, then blazing forth again. It sparked like a blazing blind eye. A wind seemed to blow from it that blistered the skin and chilled the blood.

So Argustal came to his own patch of land, clear of the green town, out in the stirring desert, and to his wife, Pamitar, to the rest of the world called Miram. She squatted with her back to the wind, the sharply flying grains of sand cutting about her hairy ankles. A few paces away, one of the beggars pranced among Argustal's stones.

Pamitar stood up slowly, removing the head shawl from her head.

'Tapmar!' she said.

Into his arms he wrapped her, burying his face in her shoulder. They chirped and clucked at each other, so engrossed that they made no note of when the breeze died and the desert lost its motion and the sun's light improved.

When she felt him tense, she held him more loosely. At a hidden signal, he jumped away from her, jumping almost over her shoulder, springing ragingly forth, bowling over the lurking beggar into the sand.

The creature sprawled, two-sided and mis-shapen, extra arms growing from arms, head like a wolf, back legs bowed like a gorilla, clothed in a hundred textures, yet not unlovely. It laughed as it rolled and called in a high clucking voice, 'Three men sprawling under a lilac tree and none to hear the first one say, "Ere the crops crawl, blows fall", and the second abed at night with mooncalves, answer me what's the name of the third, feller?'

'Be off with you, you mad old crow!'

And as the old crow ran away, it called out its answer, laughing, 'Why Tapmar, for he talks to nowhere!', confusing the words as it tumbled over the dunes and made its escape.

Argustal and Pamitar turned back to each other, vying with the strong sunlight to search out each other's faces, for both had forgotten when they were last together, so long was time, so dim was memory. But there were memories, and as he searched they came back. The flatness of her nose, the softness of her nostrils, the roundness of her eyes and their brownness, the curve of the rim of her lips: all these, because they were dear, became remembered, thus taking on more than beauty.

They talked gently to each other, all the while looking. And slowly something of that other thing he suspected on the dark side of the shield entered him – for her beloved countenance was not as it had been. Round her eyes, particularly under them, were shadows, and faint lines creased from the sides of her mouth. In her stance too, did not the lines flow more downward than heretofore?

The discomfort growing too great, he was forced to speak to Pamitar of these things, but there was no proper way to express them, and she seemed not to understand, unless she understood and did not know it, for her manner grew agitated, so that he soon forwent questioning, and turned to the parapatterner to hide his unease.

It stretched over a mile of sand, and rose several feet into the air. From each of his long expeditions, he brought back no more than five stones, yet there were assembled here many hundreds of thousands of stones, perhaps millions, all painstakingly arranged, so that no being could take in the arrangement from any one position, not even Argustal. Many were supported in the air at various heights by stakes or poles, more lay on the ground, where Pamitar always kept the dust and the wild men from encroaching them, and of these on the ground, some stood isolated, while others lay in profusion, but all in a pattern that was ever apparent only to Argustal – and he feared that it would take him until the next sunset to have that pattern clear in his head again. Yet already it started to come clearer, and he recalled with wonder the devious and fugal course he had taken, walking down to the ravine of the tree-men of Or, and knew that he still contained the skill to place the new stones he had brought within the general pattern with reference to that natural harmony – completing the parapatterner.

And the lines on his wife's face: would they too have a place within the pattern?

Was there sense in what the crow beggar had cried, that he talked to nowhere? And ... and ... the terrible and, would nowhere answer him?

Bowed, he took his wife's arm, and scurried back with her to their home, high in the leafless tree.

'My Tapmar,' she said that evening, as they ate a dish of fruit, 'it is good that you come back to Gornilo, for the town sedges up with dreams like an old river bed, and I am afraid.'

At this he was secretly alarmed, for the figure of speech she used seemed to him an apt one for the newly-observed lines on her face, so that he asked her what the dreams were in a voice more timid than he meant to use.

Looking at him strangely, she said, 'The dreams are as thick as fur, so thick that they congeal my throat to tell you of them.

Last night, I dreamed I walked in a landscape that seemed to be clad in fur all round the distant horizons, fur that branched and sprouted and had sombre tones of russet and dun and black and a lustrous black-blue. I tried to resolve this strange material into the more familiar shapes of hedges and old distorted trees, but it stayed as it was, and I became ... well, I had the word in my dream that I became a *child*.'

Argustal looked aslant over the crowded vegetation of the town and said, 'These dreams may not be of Gornilo but of you only, Pamitar. What is *child*?'

'There's no such thing in reality, to my knowledge, but in the dream the child that was I was small and fresh and in its actions at once nimble and clumsy. It was alien from me, its motions and ideas never mine – and yet it was all familiar to me, I was it, Tapmar, I was that child. And now that I wake, I become sure that I once was such a thing as a *child*.'

He tapped his fingers on his knees, shaking his head and blinking in a sudden anger. 'This is your bad secret, Pamitar! I knew you had one the moment I saw you! I read it in your face which has changed in an evil way! You know you were never anything but Pamitar in all the millions of years of your life, and that *child* must be an evil phantom that possesses you. Perhaps you will now be turned into *child*!'

She cried out and hurled a green fruit into which she had bitten. Deftly, he caught it before it struck him.

They made a provisional peace before settling for sleep. That night, Argustal dreamed that he also was small and vulnerable and hardly able to manage the language; his intentions were like an arrow and his direction clear.

Waking, he sweated and trembled, for he knew that as he had been *child* in his dream, so he had been *child* once in life. And this went deeper than sickness. When his pained looks directed themselves outside, he saw the night was like shot silk, with a dappled effect of light and shadow in the dark blue dome of the sky, which signified that the Forces were making merry with the sun while it journeyed through the Earth; and Argustal thought of his journeys across the Earth, and of his visit to Or, when the tree-men had whispered of an unknown element that forces change.

'They prepared me for this dream!' he muttered. He knew

now that change had worked in his very foundations; once, he had been this thin tiny alien thing called *child*, and his wife too, and possibly others. He thought of that little apparition again, with its spindly legs and piping voice; the horror of it chilled his heart; he broke into prolonged groans that all Pamitar's comforting took a long part of the dark to silence.

He left her sad and pale. He carried with him the stones he had gathered on his journey, the odd-shaped one from the ravine at Or and the ones he had acquired before that. Holding them tightly to him, Argustal made his way through the town to his spatial arrangement. For so long, it had been his chief preoccupation; today, the long project would come to completion; yet because he could not even say why it had so preoccupied him, his feelings inside lay flat and wretched. Something had got to him and killed content.

Inside the prospects of the parapatterner, the old beggarly man lay, resting his shaggy head on a blue stone. Argustal was too low in spirit to chase him away.

'As your frame of stones will frame words, the words will come forth stones,' cried the creature.

'I'll break your bones, old crow!' growled Argustal, but inwardly he wondered at this vile crow's saying and at what he had said the previous day about Argustal's talking to nowhere, for Argustal had discussed the purpose of his structure with nobody, not even Pamitar. Indeed, he had not recognized the purpose of the structure himself until two journeys back – or had it been three or four? The pattern had started simply as a pattern (hadn't it?) and only much later had the obsession become a purpose.

To place the new stones correctly took time. Wherever Argustal walked in his great framework, the old crow followed, sometimes on two legs, sometimes on four. Other personages from the town collected to stare, but none dared step inside the perimeter of the structure, so that they remained far off, like little stalks growing on the margins of Argustal's mind.

Some stones had to touch, others had to be just apart. He walked and stooped and walked, responding to the great pattern that he now knew contained a universal law. The task wrapped him round in an aesthetic daze similar to the one he had experienced travelling the labyrinthine way down to Or, but with greater intensity.

The spell was broken only when the old crow spoke from a few paces away in a voice level and unlike his usual sing-song. And the old crow said, 'I remember you planting the very first of these stones here when you were a child.'

Argustal straightened.

Cold took him, though the bilious sun shone bright. He could not find his voice. As he searched for it, his gaze went across to the eyes of the beggar-man, festering in his black forehead.

'You know I was once such a phantom – a child?' he asked.

'We are all phantoms. We were all childs. As there is gravy in our bodies, our hours were once few.'

'Old crow ... you describe a different world – not ours!'

'Very true, very true. Yet that other world once was ours.'

'Oh, not! Not so!'

'Speak to your machine about it! Its tongue is of rock and cannot lie like mine.'

He picked up a stone and flung it. 'That will I do! Now get away from me!'

The stone hit the old man in his ribs. He groaned painfully and danced backwards, tripped, was up again, and made off in haste, limbs whirling in a way that took from him all resemblance to human kind. He pushed through the line of watchers and was gone.

For a while, Argustal squatted where he was, groping through matters that dissolved as they took shape, only to grow large when he dismissed them. The storm blew through him and distorted him, like the trouble on the face of the sun. When he decided there was nothing for it but to complete the para-patterner, still he trembled with the new knowledge: without being able to understand why, he knew that the new knowledge would destroy the old world.

All now was in position, save for the odd-shaped stone from Or, which he carried firm on one shoulder, tucked between ear and hand. For the first time, he realized what a gigantic structure he had wrought. It was a business-like stroke of insight, no sentiment involved. Argustal was now no more than a bead rolling through the vast interstices around him.

Each stone held its own temporal record as well as its spacial position; each represented different stresses, different epochs, different temperatures, materials, chemicals, moulds, intensities. Every stone together represented an anagram of Earth, its whole composition and continuity. The last stone was merely a focal point for an entire dynamic and, as Argustal slowly walked between the vibrant arcades, that dynamic rose to pitch.

He heard it grow. He paused. He shuffled now this way, now that. As he did so, he recognized that there was no one focal position but a myriad, depending on position and direction of the key stone.

Very softly, he said '... That my fears might be verified....'

And all about him – but softly – came a voice in stone, stuttering before it grew clearer, as if it had long known of words but never practised them.

'Thou....' Silence, then a flood of sentence.

'Thou thou art, O thou art worm thou art sick, rose invisible rose. In the howling storm thou art in the storm. Worm thou art found out O rose thou art sick and found out flies in the night they bed they thy crimson life destroy. O – O rose, thou art sick! The invisible worm, the invisible worm that flies in the night, in the howling storm, has found out – has found out thy bed of crimson joy ... and his dark dark secret love, his dark secret love does thy life destroy.'

Argustal was already running from that place.

In Pamitar's arms he could find no comfort now. Though he huddled there, up in the encaging branches, the worm that flies worked in him. Finally, he rolled away from her and said, 'Who ever heard so terrible a voice? I cannot speak again with the universe.'

'You do not know it was the universe.' She tried to tease him. 'Why should the universe speak to little Tapmar?'

'The old crow said I spoke to nowhere. Nowhere is the universe – where the sun hides at night – where our memories hide, where our thoughts evaporate. I cannot talk with it. I must hunt out the old crow and talk to him.'

'Talk no more, ask no more questions! All you discover brings you misery! Look – you will no longer regard me, your poor wife! You turn your eyes away!'

'If I stare at nothing for all succeeding eons, yet I must find out what torments us!'

In the centre of Gornilo, where many of the Unclassified lived, bare wood twisted up from the ground like fossilized sack, creating caves and shelters and strange limbs on which and in which old pilgrims, otherwise without a home, might perch. Here at nightfall Argustal sought out the beggar.

The old fellow was stretched painfully beside a broken pot, clasping a woven garment across his body. He turned in his small cell, trying for escape, but Argustal had him by the throat and held him still.

'I want your knowledge, old crow!'

'Get it from the religious men – they know more than I!'

It made Argustal pause, but he slackened his grip on the other by only the smallest margin.

'Because I have you, you must speak to me. I know that knowledge is pain, but so is ignorance once one has sensed its presence. Tell me more about childs and what they did!'

As if in a fever, the old crow rolled about under Argustal's grip. He brought himself to say, 'What I know is so little, so little, like a blade of grass in a field. And like blades of grass are the distant bygone times. Through all those times come the bundles of bodies now on this Earth. Then as now, no new bodies. But once ... even before those bygone times ... you cannot understand....'

'I understand well enough.'

'You are Scientist! Before bygone times was another time, and then ... then was childs and different things that are not any longer, many animals and birds and smaller things with frail wings unable to carry them over long time...'

'What happened? Why was there change, old crow?'

'Men ... scientists ... make understanding of the gravy of bodies and turn every person and thing and tree to eternal life. We now continue from that time, a long time long – so long we forgotten what was then done.'

The smell of him was like an old pie. Argustal asked him, 'And why now are no childs?'

'Childs are just small adults. We are adults, having become from child. But in that great former time, before scientists were on Earth, adults produced childs. Animals and trees likewise. But with eternal life, this cannot be – those child-making parts of the body have less life than stone.'

'Don't talk of stone! So we live forever.... You old ragbag, you remember – ah, you remember me as child?'

But the old ragbag was working himself into a kind of fit, pummelling the ground, slobbering at the mouth.

'Seven shades of lilac, even worse I remember myself a child, running like an arrow, air, everywhere fresh rosy air. So I am mad, for I remember!' He began to scream and cry, and the outcasts round about took up the wail in chorus. 'We remember, we remember!' – whether they did or not.

Their dreadful howling worked like spears in Argustal's flank. He had pictures afterwards of his panic run through the town, of wall and trunk and ditch and road, but it was all as insubstantial at the time as the pictures afterwards. When he finally fell to the ground panting, he was unaware of where he lay, and everything was nothing to him until the religious howling had died into silence.

Then he saw he lay in the middle of his great structure, his cheek against the Or stone where he had dropped it. And as his attention came to it, the great structure round him answered without his having to speak.

He was at a new focal point. The voice that sounded was new, as cool as the previous one had been choked. It blew over him in a cool wind.

'There is no amaranth on this side of the grave, O Argustal, no name with whatsoever emphasis of passionate love repeated that is not mute at last. Experiment X gave life for eternity to every living thing on Earth, but even eternity is punctuated by release and suffers period. The old life had its childhood and its end, the new had no such logic. It found its own after many millennia, and took its cue from individual minds. What a man was, he became; what a tree, it became.'

Argustal lifted his tired head from its pillow of stone. Again the voice changed pitch and trend, as if in response to his minute gesture.

'The present is a note in music. That note can no longer be sustained. You find what questions you have found, O Argustal, because the chord, in dropping to a lower key, rouses you from the long dream of crimson joy that was immortality. What you are finding, others also find, and you can none of you be any longer insensible to change. Even immortality must have an end.'

He stood up then, and hurled the Or stone. It flew, fell, rolled ... and before it stopped he had awoken a great chorus of universal voice.

The whole Earth roused, and a wind blew from the west. As he started again to move, he saw the religious men of the town were on the march, and the great sun-nesting Forces on their midnight wing, and the stars wheeling, and every majestic object alert as it had never been.

But Argustal walked slowly on his flat simian feet, plodding back to Pamitar. No longer would he be impatient in her arms. There, time would be all too brief.

He knew now the worm that flew and nestled in her cheek, in his cheek, in all things, even in the tree-men of Or, even in the great impersonal Forces that despoiled the sun, even in the sacred bowels of the universe to which he had lent a temporary tongue. He knew now that back had come that Majesty that previously gave to Life its reason, the Majesty that had been away from the world for so long and yet so brief a respite, the Majesty called DEATH.

My first job of work as a young man was in the spaceship yards, where I felt my talents and expertise could be put to the greatest benefit of society. I worked as a FTL-fitter's mate's assistant. The FTL-fitter's mate was a woman called Nellie. As more and more women came to be employed in the yards, among the men and the androids and the robots, the men became increasingly circumspect in their behaviour. Their oaths were more guarded, their gestures less uncouth, and their care for their appearance less negligent. This I found strange, since the women showed clearly that they cared nothing for oaths, gestures, or appearances.

From wastebaskets round the site, I collected many suicide notes. Most of them had never reached their recipients and were mere drafts of suicide notes:

My darling – When you receive this, I shall no longer be in a position to ever trouble you again.

By the time you receive this letter, I shall never be able.

By the time you receive this, I shall be no more.

My darling – Never again will we be able to break each other's hearts.

You have been more than life to me. My love – I have been so wrong.

It is very good of people to take such care of their compositions even in extremis. Education has had its effect. At my school, we learnt only how to write business letters. With reference to your last shipment of Martian pig iron/iron pigs. Since life is such a tragic business, why are we not educated how to write decent suicide notes?

In this age of progress, where everything is progressive and technological and new, the only bit of our Self we have left to ourselves is our Human Condition – which of course remains miserable, despite three protein-full meals a day. Protein does not help the Dark Night of the Soul. Androids, which look so like us (we have the new Negro androids working in the space-ship yards now) do not have a soul, and many of them are very distressed at lacking the long slow toothache of the Human Condition. Some of them have left their employment, and stand on street corners wearing dark glasses, begging for alms with pathetic messages round their shoulders. Orphan of Technology. Left Factry Too Yung. Have Pity on My Poor Metal Frame. And an especially heart-wrenching one I saw in the Queens district. Obsolescence Is the Poor Man's Death. They have their traumas; just to be deprived of the Human Condition must be traumatic.

Most androids hate the android-beggars. They tour the streets after work, beating up any beggars they find, kicking their tin mugs into the gutter. Faceless androids are scaring. The look like men in iron masks. You can never escape role-playing.

We were building Q-line ships when I was in the shipyard. They were the experimental ones. The Q1, the Q2, the Q3, had each been completed, had been towed out into orbit beyond Mars, and triggered off towards Alpha Centauri. Nothing was ever heard of them again. Perhaps they are making a tour of the entire universe, and will return to the solar system when the sun is ten kilometres deep in permafrost. Anyhow, I shan't live to see the day.

It was no fun building those ships. They had no luxury, no living quarters, no furnishings, no galleys, no miles and miles of carpeting and all the other paraphernalia of a proper spaceship. There was very little we could take as supplementary income. The computers that crewed them lived very austere lives.

'The sun will be ten kilometres deep in permafrost by the time you get back to the solar system!' I told BALL, the computer on the Q3, as we walled him in. 'What will you do then?'

'I shall measure the permafrost.'

I've noticed that about the truth. You don't expect it, so it often sounds like a joke. Computers and robots sound funny quite often because they have no roles to play. They just tell the truth. I asked this BALL, 'Who will you be measuring this permafrost for?'

'I shall be measuring it for its intrinsic interest.'

'Even if there are no human beings around to be interested?'

'You misunderstand the meaning of intrinsic.'

Each of these Q ships cost more than the entire annual national income of a state like Great Britain. Zip, out into the universe they went. Never seen again! My handiwork. All those miles of beautiful seamless welding. My life's work.

I say computers tell the truth. It is only the truth as they see it. Things go on that none of us see. Should we include them in our personal truth or not?

My mother was a good old sport. Before I reached the age of ten and was given my extra-familial posting, she and I had a lot of fun. Hers was a heart of gold – more, of uranium. She had an old deaf friend called Mrs. Patt who used to come and visit mother once a week and sit in the big armchair while mother yelled questions and remarks at her.

Now I realize why I could not bear Mrs. Patt – because everything I said sounded so trivial and stupid when repeated at the top of my voice.

'It's nice about the extra moonlight law, isn't it?'

'You what you say?'

'I said aren't you pleased about the extra moonlight law?'

'Pleased what?'

'Aren't you pleased about the extra moonlight law? We could do with another moon.'

'I can't hear what you say.'

'I say isn't it fun about the extra moonlight law?'

'What lawn is that?'

'The extra moonlight law. Law! Isn't it fun about the extra moonlight law?'

I used to hide behind the armchair before Mrs. Patt came in. When she and mother started shouting, I would rise over the back of the chair so that Mrs. Patt could not see me, sticking my thumbs in my ears and my little fingers up my nostrils so that my nose was wrinkled and distorted, waving my other fingers about while shooting my brows up and down, flobbing my tongue, and blinking my eyes furiously, in order to make mother laugh. She had to pretend she could not see me.

Occasionally, she would have to pretend to blow her nose, in order to enjoy a quick chuckle.

We had a big bad black cat. Sometimes I would appear round the chair with the tom dish on my head, mewing and wagging my ears.

The question I now ask myself, having reached more sober years – Mrs. Patt visited the euthanasia clinic years ago – is whether I should or should not be included among Mrs. Patt's roll call of truths. Since I was not among her observable phenomena, then I could not be part of her revealed Truth. For Mrs. Patt, I did not exist in my post-armchair manifestation; therefore my effect upon her Self was totally negligible; therefore I could form no portion of her Truth, as she saw it.

Whether what I was doing was well- or ill-intentioned towards her likewise did not matter, since it did not impinge on her consciousness. The only effect of my performance on her was that she came to consider my mother as someone unusually prone to colds, necessitating frequent nose-blowing.

This suggests that there are two sorts of truth : one's personal truth, and what, for fear of using an even more idiotic term, I will call a Universal Truth. In this last category clearly belong events that go on even if nobody is observing them, like my fingers up my nose, the flights of the Q1, Q2, and Q3, and God.

All this I once tried to explain to my android friend, Jackson. I tried to tell him that he could only perceive Universal Truth, and had no cognizance of Personal Truth.

'Universal Truth is the greater, so I am greater than you, who perceives only Personal Truth,' he said.

'Not at all! I obviously perceive all of Personal Truth, since that's what it means, and also quite a bit of Universal Truth. So I get a much better idea of Total Truth than you.'

'Now you are inventing a third sort of truth, in order to win the argument. Just because you have Human Condition, you have to keep proving you are better than me.'

I switched him off. I am better than Jackson. I can switch him off.

Next day, going back on shift, I switched him on again.

'There are all sorts of horrible things signalling behind your metaphorical armchair that you aren't aware of,' he said immediately.

'At least human beings write suicide notes,' I said. It is a minor art that has never received full recognition. A very intimate art. You can't write a suicide note to someone you do not know.

'Dear President – My name may not be familiar to you but I voted for you in the last election and, when you receive this, I shall no longer be able to trouble you ever again.'

'I shall no longer ever be able to vote for you again. Not be able to support you at the next election.'

'Dear President – This will come as something of a shock, particularly since you don't know me, but.'

'Dear Sir – You have been more than a president to me.'

The hours in the spaceship yards were long, particularly for us young lads. We worked from ten till twelve and again from two till four. The robots worked from ten till four. The androids worked from ten till twelve and from two till four when I began at the yards as a FTL-fitter's mate's assistant, and they had no breaks for canteen, whereas men and women got fifteen minutes off in every hour for coffee and drugs. After I had been in the yards for some ten months, legislation was passed allowing androids five minutes off in every hour for coffee (they don't take drugs). The men went on strike against this legislation, but it all simmered down by Christmas, after a pay rise. The Q4 was delayed another sixteen weeks, but what is sixteen weeks when you are going to go round the universe?

The women were very emotional. Many of them fell in love with androids. The men were very bitter about this. My first love, Nellie, the FTL-fitter's mate, left me for an android electrician. She said he was more respectful.

In the canteen, we men used to talk about sex and philosophy and who was winning the latest Out-Thinking Contest. The women used to exchange recipes. I often feel women do not have quite such a large share of the Human Condition as we do.

When we first went to bed together Nellie said, 'You're a bit nervous, aren't you?'

Well, I was, but I said, 'No, I'm not nervous, it's just this question of role-playing. I haven't entirely devised one to cover this particular situation.'

'Well, buck up, then, or the whistle will be going. You can be the Great Lover or something, can't you?'

'Do I look like the Great Lover?' I asked in exasperation.

'I've seen smaller,' she said, and she smiled. After that, we always got on well together, and then she had to leave me for that android electrician.

For a few days, I was terribly miserable. I thought of writing her a suicide note but I didn't know how to word it.

'Dear Nellie – I know you are too hard-hearted to care a hoot about this, but. I know you don't care a hoot but. I know you don't give a hoot. Give a rap. Are indifferent to. Are indifferent to what happens to me, but.

'As you lie there in the synthetic arms of your lover, it may interest you to know I am about to.'

But I was not really about to, for I struck up a close friendship with Nancy, and she enjoyed my Great Lover role. She was very good with an I-Know-We're-Really-Both-Too-Sensible-For-This role. After a time, I got a transfer so that I could work with her on the starboard condentister. She used to tell me recipes for exotic dishes. Sometimes, it was quite a relief to get back to my mates in the canteen.

At last the great day came when the Q4 was finished. The President came down and addressed us, and inspected the two-mile-high needle of shining steel. He told us it had cost more than all South America was worth, and would open up a New Era in the History of mankind. Or perhaps he said New Error. Anyhow, the Q4 was going to put us in touch with some other civilization, many light years away. It was imperative for our survival that we get in rapport with them before our enemies did.

'Why don't we just get in rapport with our enemies?' Nancy asked me sourly. She has no sense of occasion.

As we all came away from the ceremony, I had a nasty surprise. I saw Nellie with her arm round that android electrician, and he was limping. An android, limping! There's role-playing for you. Byronic androids! If we aren't careful, they will be taking over the Human Condition just as they are taking our women. The future is black and the bins of our destiny are filling with suicide notes.

I felt really sick. Nancy stared at me as if she could see someone over my shoulder putting his thumbs in his ears and his little fingers up his nose and all that. Of course, when I looked round, nobody was there.

'Let's go and play Great Lovers while there's still time,' I said.

Swastika!

On 30th April 1945, in his bunker in the Berlin Chancellory, Adolf Hitler crunched an ampoule of potassium cyanide. Then he was shot through the head by Heinz Linge, his valet, and his body taken out into the garden of the Chancellory and burnt – or partially burnt.

Some of these 'facts' were known almost immediately. Luckily, the Soviet force got to the scene of the crime first and, only twenty-three years later, rushed out the rest of the facts. The one thing that makes me doubt the truth of the whole account is that I happen to know Hitler is alive and well and living in Ostend under the assumed name – at least, I assume it is assumed – of Geoffrey Bunglevester.

I was over to see him last week, before the winter became too advanced. Of course, he is getting on in years now, but is amazingly spry for his age and still takes an interest in politics, supporting the Flems against the Walloons.

As we usually did, we met in a cosy little bar not too distant from where he lived. We had been talking business but gradually turned to more personal matters.

'Looking back,' I said, 'do you ever have any regrets?'

'I wish I'd done more with my painting.' A far-off look came into his eyes. 'Landscape painting – that would have suited me. I flatter myself I always had an eye for pretty landscapes.' He started reeling off their names: the Rhineland, Austria, Czechoslovakia, Poland.... To keep him to the subject, I said, 'I'd certainly agree that some of your early water-colours showed astonishing promise, but haven't you ever regretted – well, any of your military judgements?'

He looked me straight in the eye, brushing his forelock back to do so.

'You're not getting at me, Brian, are you? You're not trying to be sarcastic at my expense?'

'No, honestly, Geoff, why should I?'

He leant over the table towards me and glanced over one shoulder.

'You are Aryan, aren't you?'

'I went to an English public school, if that's what you mean.'

'That's good enough for me. Very fine unrivalled disciplinary system! Well, I apologize, I thought you were trying to get at me for attempting to apply a final solution to the Jewish problem.'

'It never entered my head, Geoff.'

'Very well, only I'm a little touchy on that score, you see. I've been very unfairly criticized there ever since the Third Reich collapsed in 1945. You see, there was a much deeper intention behind the extermination of the Jews; *that* was little but a warming-up exercise to get the machinery going. The ultimate target – the course on which I was intending to embark by 1950 at the latest, before I was so rudely interrupted – was the extermination of the Negro races.'

I gasped as the enormity of his plan came home to me.

'Surely – surely, an error in tactics —' I began falteringly. In his almost boyish eagerness, he misunderstood what I was going to say. Leaning forward over the table, his eyes shining, he said, 'Yes, perhaps it was an error in tactics – you see, I admit I commit errors occasionally – not to have announced my grand plan to the world. Then the Americans would have been sympathetic and stayed out of the war. Well, too late now to cry over spilt milk. . . . If only I could have pulled off the eradication of the Negroes, admittedly it would have seemed rather controversial to begin with; but afterwards I would have been accepted, I think it's fair to say, as a benefactor.'

'Except by the Negroes themselves?'

He took my naïvety in good part.

'My dear boy, even the Negroes themselves admit that nobody likes them. I would merely have followed that through to its logical conclusion. Heaven knows, I've never courted popularity for its own sake, but you yourself would admit that I've had to put up with more than my share of backbiting. Even the German people have to pretend to have turned against me.'

He shook his head, looking very downcast. To console him, I said, 'Well, Geoff, that's the unfair way the world treats the defeated – there's no respect for ambition nowadays —'

'Defeated! Who was defeated? Have you fallen victim to all the lying Jewish bourgeois bolshevik anti-Nazi propaganda too? I've not been defeated —'

'But surely in 1945 —'

'What happened in 1945 is neither here nor there! It just happens to be the year when I chose to step back and let others take over the arduous role of waging war and waking whole populations from their slave-mentality inertia.'

'You don't mean – you're claiming a sort of psychological victory? A —'

He poured us both another measure of red wine and watered it down with mineral water. 'It was my old racist enemies who spread the lie that peace broke out in 1945. It is not true – what old Winston would call a terminological inexactitude, in his comic way. That was the year the Americans dropped the first A-bomb and started the nuclear arms race which shows no sign of slackening yet, particularly now that the U.S.A. and U.S.S.R. have managed to goad China into joining the competition. *We* hadn't the resources to manufacture war material on that scale, alas!'

'But you can't compare the Cold War with World War II, Adolf!'

'Geoff to you, Brian.'

'Geoff, I mean. Sorry.'

'I'm not comparing. The one *developed* from the other; 1945 saw the change from one phase to the next. The continuity is clear. Look at the Russians! I don't think much of the Slav races, but you have to hand it to them – their policy of aggression has been consistent for half a century now. I don't know if you recall the name of Joseph Stalin? A bit of a rogue, but a man after my own heart. He told me back in – oh, 1938, I think it would be, that he would like to get into Europe —'

'The Common Market —'

'And of course he did so and, only this year, his followers are still obeying his orders and marching into Czechoslovakia just as I did, way back!' He clapped his thigh with genuine pleasure. 'That was the time! – A ball, as today's youngsters would say! Beautiful city, Prague! The sun shining, the Wehrmacht in their best uniforms, the tanks rolling, everyone shouting "Heil—" ... well, Heil Me, let's say, and the pretty Czech girls hanging flowers round our necks....' The mood of genial reminiscence softened his rather harsh profile. 'You were only a boy then, Brian....'

'I can remember the occasion, all the same. But the Russian invasion of Czechoslovakia in 1968 is a different thing —'

'It's still part of World War II, just like the Korean War and Vietnam and the Middle East hot-pot. They are all conflagrations lit from the torch I started burning in Europe.' It was a concept almost beyond my grasping, and I told him as much.

'I'll have to beg to differ there. After all, the 1945 peace treaties —'

'I've no wish to be unpleasant, but I was slightly more in the centre of things than you were, after all. I'm sure that General Curtis Le May or your Viscount "Monty" don't think of the war as being over, not by a long chalk. Men like that, strong men, men born with iron in their bones, they all have something of Bismarck in them – they hold the great vision of peace as merely a time for re-arming. How's the drink? More mineral water?'

I covered my glass with my hand. 'No, thanks, just right. Well, we mustn't argue —'

'Excuse me, we must argue if you do not accept my point. My war, as I pardonably regard it, is still being waged, is breaking out afresh, and may soon even return to its fatherland. What does it all mean if not victory for me and my ideals?'

Moved if not convinced, I felt I was in touch with greatness.

'Always the old warrior, Geoff! You've never despaired, have you?'

'Despair! Who can afford to despair? Besides, the world has given me little real cause for despair. Men of warrior caste are still alive everywhere.'

'I suppose so. But I was a bit surprised by what you were saying just now about General Le May. I understood that you basically had little respect for the American spirit?'

Sipping his drink, he looked at me with reproach in his eyes.

'Let's be fair to the Americans. I know as well as you do that their whole continent is over-run by a rabble of Slavs and Jews and Mexicans and Spaniards and the sweepings of Africa and Scandinavia; but fortunately there is a backbone of Teutonic and Anglo-Saxon military morale there too. They aren't all semi-Asiatic ghetto-infesting-decadents like Roosevelt. I know a back-street racially-inferior lackey-mentality has often prevailed in the past, but just recently a more upright no-nonsense element is coming to the fore and triumphing over the flabby democratic processes. I have been extremely encouraged to see the vigorous uncompromising attitudes of American leaders like Reagan and Governor Wallace. President Nixon also has his better side. Of course, the American practice-war in Vietnam is hopelessly ill-run and . . .'

'Namby-pamby?'

'Yes, good, namby-pamby . . . Namby-pamby. Except for poor old de Gaulle, the French are namby-pamby, eh? What was I saying? Yes, a more realistic spirit growing in America. They failed in logic by hesitating to use thermonuclear weapons in Vietnam, but that obscurantist attitude is altering and soon I expect to see them employing such solutions to restore discipline within their own frontiers.'

'Incurably the grand strategist!' I smiled. 'Do you find yourself reliving your old campaigns over and over?'

'I don't think so, not more than most people. Himmler was terribly sentimental, but not I. I'd say I was a pretty average sort of person. I like to keep up with current events. A friend in England sends me *The Times* every day. And, as I believe I told you, I'm now writing some poetry.' He smiled modestly, with a twitch of his moustache.

'Don't know how you'll take this, Geoff, but do you think I could possibly see some of your poetry some time? Just take a peek at it?'

He sat back and looked at me, half-laughing – yet I thought there was a mist in his eyes, as if my interest had touched him.

'What possible interest could an old man's poetry have for you?'

Perhaps the watered-down wine was having its due effect. Hunching my shoulders over the table, I said, 'You can hardly imagine what a deep impression you made on me when I was a kid, Geoff. In England, we never had a strong leader like you in the thirties and, by god, we desperately need one again now – Harold Wilson's much too mild and permissive! I – okay, I know it sounds sentimental – but you were a father-figure to me, Geoff, and to thousands like me who had the luck to fight in the war. All those marvellous torch-light processions you used to have, and the shouting, and the beautiful deep-bosomed frauleins, and the way your troops kept so faultlessly in step! And then the dramatic way you just swept across Europe in the late thirties and early forties.... It was wonderful to watch! I mean, it didn't *matter* that we were on opposite sides; we knew you were really a friend of the British Empire.'

'A better friend to you than the decadent Americans proved.' He looked down at his glass, and I could not help but note the tired lines round his mouth. 'Yes, Brian, those were great days, no denying that. You needn't reproach yourself for feeling as you do about them. Nobody's in quite the same class today – the Russians, the South Africans, the Rhodesians, the Portuguese. ... They're just not in the same class.'

He shook his head. For a moment, we were both too full of emotion to speak, wondering perhaps if the great days of Earth were not gone for ever. Then I asked, softly, 'Do you ever wish things had worked out differently, Geoff? I mean – for you personally?'

I shall never forget his answer. He didn't look up, just went on clutching his glass with hands that shook slightly (his old disease still troubled him occasionally) and staring down at the wine.

In a voice from which he strove to hold back tears, he said, 'I'm getting old and sentimental, as you know. But sometimes I despair of the world ever getting put to rights. The permanent East–West confrontation is well enough, and the two mutually inter-dependent persecution manias of America and Russia have served to maintain the world's battle-alertness over some otherwise lack-lustre years. But ...'

He sighed. No man should look as isolated as he did at that minute. He resembled a mystic staring down a telescope the wrong way at a golden dream.

'But ...' I prompted. 'You had a master plan?'

'I've had emissaries come to me over the years, Brian. I may as well tell you. They come humbly to me, exiled here in Ostend. Soviet and American – and British too, to begin with. They've come swarming to me in secret. Yes, and the little tinpot rulers too. Nasser, Papa Doc, that Rhodesian fellow – Jones? Smith? – that ingrate Chou En Lai, Castro – filthy little Communist! All on their knees here! Even – yes, even General Dayan of Israel. Not a bad fellow, considering.... They've all begged me to take charge of their war aims, clarify them, implement them. "You can have the whole Pacific if you'll help me take Peking". That's what – h'm, memory's going – Soekarno said. Always it was *me* they wanted. It's the old charisma....'

'Either you've got it or you haven't,' I agreed. 'Why didn't you accept their offers – America's and Russia's, I mean?'

'Because the imbeciles asked me to rule them and yet wouldn't give me full power!' He struck the table with his fist. 'They wanted me and yet they were afraid of me! LBJ and I met in this very café ... person to person – remember LBJ? This is confidential, mind you, and I don't want it to go any further.'

'You can trust me,' I assured him fervently. My eyes were starting out of my head. 'You actually met LBJ here?'

'He paid for the drinks. Insisted on it. Rather big-mouthed, said his wife had sent him! He was in trouble with the Communists abroad and the Negroes and white-trash subversive crypto-mulatto elements at home. Would I help him? I said I would. With me in charge, the United States could have conquered the world. Not a doubt of it! Russia first – use up all those rusty old H-bombs! pffft! – then Europe invaded and rationalized. Then the rest of the world would just be erased, wiped clean, starting probably with South America. Wiped clean. Nothing namby-pamby.'

'Why didn't LBJ take you up on it? It sounds like his big chance!'

'If you can believe it, he had some hare-brained scheme for preserving India from destruction. He was a yellow liberal at heart and the deal fell through.'

I was aghast. 'Why should anyone wish to preserve India from destruction, India of all places?'

'My dear man, American colonialist ambitions are as much of a mystery to me as to you! A pity – together, or preferably me alone, we could have built a tidier world, an altogether tidier world where people would have to do EXACTLY WHAT THEY ARE TOLD TO DO!'

'Cowardice is at the bottom of it all,' I said, after a pause. 'During the war, we had group leadership and bombing raids and discipline, and people all worked hard. Now we're stuck with the permissive society.'

He was following his own line of thought. It was a moment or two before he spoke again and I could see the bar was about to close.

'I'm getting old and sentimental, as you know, Brian. But I begin to wish more and more that I had conquered England instead of Poland. It's a prettier part of the world. The people are nicer. I could have settled down in Torquay or somewhere and married a nice pure English girl. But there ... it wasn't meant to be. No use being sentimental....'

It was time for him to go. We trudged back to his flat together through the streets of Ostend. He was wearing his old grey trench coat which still bore the swastikas he had never bothered to remove. What symbols of nostalgia they were! In a flash I had found a title for the musical of his life which I had come to discuss with him: 'Swastika!' Of course! 'Swastika!' I shall always think of that moment as one of the most dramatic in my whole life, the war notwithstanding.

We halted on his doorstep.

'I won't ask you in,' he said. 'The concierge is down with flu.' He always referred to Martin Bormann as 'the concierge', in his humorous way.

'It's been wonderful talking to you,' I said.

'I've enjoyed it, too,' he said. 'And I promise to come over to London for the première – provided that Jewish chap doesn't write the music.'

'Count on me,' I said simply. 'And don't forget – two-and-a-half per cent of the gross.'

We eyed one another in complete understanding. For sentiment's sake, I knew how I wanted to bid him good-bye; but there were people passing, and I was a little embarrassed. Instead, I grasped his worn frail hand in both of mine.

'Good-bye, Geoffrey!'

'Auf wiedersehen, Brian, dear boy!'

Blinking moisture from my eyes, I hurried for the airport, the contract in my pocket.

Acknowledgements

My thanks go to the editors of the magazines and anthologies in which the stories concerned first appeared: *Moment of Eclipse* and ... *And the Stagnation of the Heart* in New Worlds; *The Day We Embarked for Cythera* in Nova; *Orgy of the Living and the Dying* in The Year 2000; *Super-Toys Last All Summer Long* in Harper's Bazaar; *The Village Swindler* in International; *That Uncomfortable Pause Between Life and Art* in Queen; *Down the Up Escalation* in London Magazine; *Confluence* and *Working in the Spaceship Yards* in Punch; *Heresies of the Huge God* in Galaxy; *The Circulation of the Blood* in Impulse; *The Worm that Flies* in The Farthest Reaches; *Swastika!* in Nova 1.

Other Panthers For Your Enjoyment

Asimov in Panther

☐ **THE STARS LIKE DUST**   30p
A great Utopian story of a chase through the length and breadth
of the galaxy in search of a secret document which may be the key
to the overthrow of tyranny.

☐ **THE END OF ETERNITY**   30p
Mankind is spreading through the galaxy -- and meets an alien
intelligence which is moving in from the shadowy 'outside'. How to
stop them? Simple -- you modify the past: except that nothing ever
is as simple as that in Isaac Asimov's stupendous cosmology.

☐ **THE CAVES OF STEEL**   30p
Many writers have tried to merge science fiction with the
detective story, but only Asimov has supremely succeeded.
THE CAVES OF STEEL has a detective -- an unusual one --
operating in the deep-down warrens of an over-populated metropolis
-- and if you think you know what over-population means . . . read
Asimov.

☐ **THE NAKED SUN**   30p
Another science fiction/detective story masterpiece. A tec from
over-crowded Earth has to take off to a sparsely populated
way-out planet. After the teeming dens of Earth -- a sort of womb
existence -- the wide open spaces make him literally sick.
Nevertheless, there's a killer on the loose -- to be run down.

☐ **ASIMOV'S MYSTERIES**   30p
Short, sharp stories about murders, mayhems, crooks and
detectives fouling up Asimov's cleanly organised science fiction
worlds. This deep, dark space collection rounds off the author's
excursion into the s.f./thriller field.

☐ **THE MARTIAN WAY**   30p
Four novellas by Asimov. The author races along -- taking Mars
in his stride (the title is a misnomer) as he slams his penetrating
imagination into the deeps of space and time.

Science Fiction

☐ **Theodore Sturgeon**   **E PLURIBUS UNICORN**   25p

Already classic but completely modern stories by a giant of
science fiction and fantasy.

☐ **D. F. Jones**   **DON'T PICK THE FLOWERS**   30p

A mohole is drilled deep through Earth's crust – and the trapped
nitrogen blows. To escape the horror two men and two girls put
out to sea – only to discover that seething nitrogen is the least of
their terrors. It's in the classic disaster story tradition of
John Wyndham.

☐ **Charles Harness**   **THE ROSE**   25p

Acclaimed by masters of SF – Brian Aldis, Arthur C. Clarke,
Michael Moorcock, Judith Merril and many others – as a
rare masterpiece.

☐ **Robert A. Heinlein**   **DOUBLE STAR**   25p

A fantastic double-take in deep space and time. A vintage example
of the unique Heinlein imagination at work. A Hugo Award winner.

☐ **Thomas M. Disch**   **ECHO ROUND HIS BONES**   25p

By the prize winning novelist whose work is *not* just for SF fans,
but for all who enjoy the modern novel. A man on the moon
meets his exact double who wishes to destroy him.

☐ **J. G. Ballard**   **THE CRYSTAL WORLD**   30p

Switch off the reality around you and voyage up an African river
into one of Ballard's fantastic futures. Accompanying are a couple
of adulterous lovers, a manic gunman and a priest who's lost his
faith in favour of a very wayout ritual indeed. But for all of them –
including the reader – universal crystallisation's what's in store.

Obtainable from all booksellers and newsagents. If you have
any difficulty please send purchase price plus 7p postage per
book to Panther Cash Sales, P.O. Box 11, Falmouth, Cornwall.

I enclose a cheque/postal order for titles ticked above plus 7p.
a book to cover postage and packing.

Name⎯⎯⎯⎯⎯⎯⎯⎯⎯⎯⎯⎯⎯⎯⎯

Address⎯⎯⎯⎯⎯⎯⎯⎯⎯⎯⎯⎯⎯

⎯⎯⎯⎯⎯⎯⎯⎯⎯⎯⎯⎯⎯⎯⎯⎯⎯⎯